Seven Loves

Seven Loves

A NOVEL

Valerie Trueblood

LITTLE, BROWN AND COMPANY
NEW YORK • BOSTON

Little, Brown and Company
Hachette Book Group USA
1271 Avenue of the Americas, New York, NY 10020

FIRST EDITION: JUNE 2006

The characters and events in this book are fictitious. Any similarity to real
persons, living or dead, is coincidental and not intended by the author.

Library of Congress Cataloging-in-Publication Data

Trueblood, Valerie.
    Seven loves : a novel / Valerie Trueblood—1st ed.
        p. cm.
    ISBN-10: 0-316-05893-9
    ISBN-13: 978-0-316-05893-3
    1. Women—Fiction. I. Title.

PS3620.R84S48 2006
813'.6—dc22   2005026604

10 9 8 7 6 5 4 3 2 1

Q-FF

Book design by Fearn Cutler de Vicq

Printed in the United States of America

Seven Loves

Intransitive: Jackie

In the café a white-haired woman is smiling at a little girl at the next table, who grins back playfully all during breakfast. The child's mother, in a suit, silk blouse, and sneakers for the walk to work, has noticed the attention to her daughter. On the way out, she says to the older woman as they pass her table, "Should we keep her?"

The woman, May, sits very still, blank. "She *is* pretty cute, isn't she?" prompts the mother in the same bright, practical voice, turning the child by the shoulders now with her fingertips. The little girl has a pointed chin, rosy cheeks, and very fair hair, frizzy and full of static. In the sun pouring through the skylight the hair sputters off her head in all directions. She's about four years old. She rolls her brown eyes, swings her lunchbox, and teeters against the mother.

It is late April, bright in the morning. Outside the window there is so much light and shade striping pavement and buses and people hurrying to work, so many pigeons flying and reflections weltering in the panes across the street, that it is confusing to look.

May has been taken by surprise. She can't move. As an ex-teacher of English, who goes at least twice a week to the movies, she prides herself on knowing city talk. *Should we keep her?* When the mother and daughter have paid their check she sits still, holding her coffee cup. They appear outside the window on the sidewalk, the little fiery-headed girl now stalking forward with her lunchbox, ahead of the mother. Down the flickering street. Farther down, the runaways are already sitting cross-legged against the Copy Center in their silver-studded black clothes. The child marches away. Not to be kept. To be traded, like Joseph into the caravan.

Why did the woman say that to May? To May, who some-times looks into the bathroom mirror in the morning, and despite what she sees at that hour, at her age, hears her mother's voice say, "You're my *real* darling."

Suddenly it's clear. The woman was joking, a commonplace joke: should we keep her? May's reaction, her incomprehension: could she have had one of those ministrokes with which her doc-tor has threatened her? She has already had a little episode at the office. She leans back, winded. If somebody says, "Should we keep her?" ever again she'll say shrewdly, "Well, I don't know, does she eat her vegetables?" Or if the child has a gleam of mis-chief in her eye, she can say with a cackle, "You give her to me, I have just the place to put her." She isn't a know-nothing old woman keeping herself occupied at breakfast as long as possible. She is on her way to work too. Some years ago she retired from teaching, but in no time at all she landed in a computer class.

Several companies in the city got together to develop the program, known as Senior Class, which won an award for returning older people to the workplace.

Her gaze falls on her hands, the nails painted—imperfectly, she sees now—a red-pink. In the position of her fingers she can read exactly what it was like to hold a cigarette. Briefly her fingers recall the texture of items in her purse as she used to shuffle them without looking, feeling for her lighter. Hypertension. A word her doctor says with a calm reproof, bony finger pointing shakily at her torso. May has, he says, folding the finger back into his palm, the barrel shape that overloads the heart. He has barred her from rummaging for the lighter. May is not really sentimental about smoking, nor does she feel any bitterness, like that of the woman who wrote a letter to the editor saying that in the long run Kents had meant more to her than either of her husbands. But May considers that she has been diminished, lost a careless power she had, to incorporate fire.

With the cigarettes went her perfect hearing. Now she hears a noise like a soft gong shadowing her speech. A definite echo, something to do with the cochlea, according to Dr. Jenkins. Drinking her coffee she decides to consider squarely whether her mind is as sound as ever, but she can think of no test to give herself, nothing that could stand for the whole of her mind and be measured, no giveaway sign like the one Patricia at work spied in her earlobe.

She has on large earrings, moons of stamped silver from Mexico, given to her by Patricia, who at fifty is the oldest in the office other than herself. "This will diversify her look," Patricia told them all, snapping the earrings onto May's ears. "Lucky for you they had clip-ons in Taxco." Patricia treats her like a plain daughter who needs to be brought out. "See this? This crease?" Patricia said, pulling off the earring and doubling May's long, passive earlobe in her fingers. "Heart. I read about it, the crease in the earlobe. You show that to your doctor. They never notice."

"I will," May said obediently.

Usually she wears pants but today she has on a belted dress with a jacket. The dress is a chic olive green, one of the best things in her closet now, saved for occasions that rarely arise. Despite her large waistline, she has worn the belt. Normally she would leave it off, having cut the belt loops from her few dresses. But in a fever of vitality last night she sat under the lamp with needle and thread, piecing a section of elastic into the belt that came with the dress and covering it with material out of the hem. She could not remember, this morning, why this had seemed such an exhilarating and fateful action.

Things like this, done increasingly in the evenings when she can't be still, are part of the condition she is in. She has analyzed it, and found it tied to a subject much dwelt on when she taught, because of her students' confusion over transitive and intransitive. "Whatever your dictionary or any dictionary of the future may say, in my class you cannot *enjoy,* you cannot *await.* You have to await *something.*" Now, she thinks, her own emotions take that prohibited form. They *await.* No object. Verb limited to the agent.

She pictures her feelings as a kind of mold. Spores, wafted from somewhere else, that come to rest in her, followed by blue splotches of mold, which begin to pool and billow. So—the furious sympathies, the weeklong fits of sleepless excitement she is prey to: mold. Perhaps she is downy and blue inside, stirring waywardly, like the child's hair under the skylight.

At seventy-four, she is in love. Or not love. What is it? A consuming interest in another person—a person of not much interest, really, she thinks in bewilderment—has seized her, so that she looks forward to even the mildest encounters at work.

She has had crushes before. They blew away in the telling, when her older daughter Laura was still nearby to hear about them, but Laura is gone; her own children have grown up and she has gone with her husband Will to live abroad. May has had a year or so to get used to that. Of the long days of packing up Laura's household she remembers only her son-in-law's voice, loud in the empty rooms. She keeps the name of the country where they live out of her conversation at work, because with it comes a gust of cold air left in their wake—though the country is warm.

She doesn't cry about Laura's move. Her feeling about it is quite a disciplined, still one, without any of the radiating, the sinuous groping, of the feelings that make up the blue mold.

Every so often at work one of the women—actually girls, several of them are still girls—will cry. It is one of the privileges of youth to cry in the ladies' room, and to be gradually coaxed out and made to say what is the matter, and to give pleasure by doing so. May remembers doing it herself, in the jobs she had during college and even in the hectic first years she taught school. At a later time, tears were to be hidden at all costs.

The sweet Jackie, the one who occupies her thoughts, is the youngest person in the office, and gives the most pleasure, with her clumsy, passionate sorrows, the elementary nature of her problems with men, which they are all eager to solve for her, and her bad luck. Jackie has the worst luck of any of them. She is looking for a good, kind man—that's all she asks—and she meets lightweights and playboys and perverts. Already, at the age of twenty-four, she has lost her two children in a custody suit. As nearly as anybody in the office can figure out, she lost them because she had them in day care, while in court her ex-husband showed the intention of hiring someone to live in to take care of them. Actually Jackie has her children most of the time, or the day care does, because her husband didn't really mean he wanted them. He meant something else. It turned out he was almost as young, confused, and clumsy as Jackie. He never hired anybody to live in, he bypassed the judge's decision and one day just gave the children back to Jackie. Still, he reserved the right to put them out of her reach if he chose.

Both children turned a grayish brown during the month he had them with him in L.A. When Jackie covered them with kisses at the airport they were grimy, salty from seawater. Their tanned skin gave off a smell. Jackie herself is clean with the cleanliness seen and felt, May thinks, only in offices like this, where there is something devotional in the women's preparations for work. "I didn't know children *had* a smell," Jackie said. "I don't think he gave them baths. I'm wondering if he knows they have to *have* baths," she said in her slow voice, remarkable for its lack of impatience. There is a melody to Jackie's speech that makes May think of Marilyn Monroe's voice of benign, very nearly pathetic, loveliness. Sometimes she wonders just where, in the eleventh-grade class she taught all those years, Jackie would have appeared in the percentiles. Can she be as ignorant as she seems?

But there is her beauty. Wherever Jackie goes, in her car, on the street, in stores, she is pointed out. In the big building their floor is known as the one where Jackie gets off the elevator. Her beauty is a pollen shaken onto all of them. She could be looking out over ruins, over oceans, a stone woman holding up a roof. She comes to life, moves along the line of cubicles to the ladies' room, stopping to speak to everybody, gracious, thinks May, as the Virgin. Though not so graceful. Jackie carries herself with a guarded slowness, but she is large-boned and awkward; she scatters paper and she tips over desk vases and coffee cups. May waits to be the one to excuse her.

Jackie is not only beautiful, she is generous. She comes to May's desk, lays a huge tissue-wrapped package on the computer monitor, and May tears off the tissue to find an afghan crocheted in turquoise, yellow, and mauve. "I just did it watching TV, it's nothing," Jackie says softly. "Now, May, I want you to wrap up in this on a rainy night. I know your place is cold." How does she know this, without having been there? Her voice is pitched low, as if to soothe a cat.

At Christmas, dusting powder and lavender soap for May, each cake in thin silver paper tied with purple ribbon. For her birthday, a quilted tea cozy.

It doesn't bother May that Jackie has made or chosen presents with the sort of hopeful, unspecific appropriateness—which is at the same time the hopeless, smiling, defeated inappropriateness— of tributes you might take with you to give your hosts in a foreign country.

Jackie has a ripe mouth and a beautiful nose, slightly puffy at the base as if from crying. She wears her golden-brown hair un- fashionably long, sometimes in a loose braid. "I gave up," she will say. "All morning I tried to get this into a French braid. It makes your arms ache. How do they do those things?" The remarkable thing is that despite her looks, all the women like her; they buy her little cards to stick up around her desk that say things like "Yes, it's still my break," and memo pads printed "To Whom It May Confuse." Jackie smiles at these offerings, but the fact is she has no humor. After six months of watching and listening, May is reasonably sure of this. To Jackie, everything is absolutely serious.

May has come under the spell of this seriousness.

What does it matter if you are stupid, she finds herself thinking, if you are beautiful and sad? If you have this sobriety about life, if you are absorbent of it, as Jackie is, if you read the newspaper every day at your desk as if it were a letter you had to answer. May has the example of her own mother, who did answer, who wrote tirelessly to editors, and tried, more fiercely than Jackie ever could, certainly, to sway any mind confused by the indifferent or the heartless: the Hoover administration, or strikebreakers, or the common opinion.

But in Jackie's case, all that is not sad confusion is secret pattern. She always reports several items at lunch: murders, implausible accidents, crimes against children, the coincidences that determine who boards doomed planes. Or she recounts stories from a book she has been reading for weeks, about near-death experiences. Unaware of May's attention, she looks out the window, her nose swollen, her dark blue eyes faraway as she describes men, women, and children from the near-death book who tore themselves out of the grasp of hands reaching from the other side, or were let go more gently because there was something left for them to accomplish.

At first, when May was new to the office, she grinned to herself whenever Jackie talked. She thought not just of her mother, who would have laughed with disbelief at the idea of a woman like Jackie who did nothing with her sympathies. She thought of her husband Cole, dead for years: how he would have enjoyed stories of Jackie. He would not have seen exactly what May meant, never having been susceptible, as May was, to the allure of an indefinable humility or an unlikely goodness or an unfocused, caressing gaze. But he would have liked the office stories; he would have been someone to whom she could tell them, with both daughters gone. Or would he? What if he could have come up, just once, in the elevator with May to this hidden office of women, where she did work of no importance in a program he and she would have laughed at together? Would he have said, *May, for God's sake, what are you doing here?* No, she liked to think he would have said, *I see.* And then, *That must be Jackie. There, the beautiful one.* But there was no way to be sure.

Then, over a month or two, May lost altitude. A series of slow drops followed, as in dreams when four or five stairs are missing as you go down. She began to note the times of Jackie's trips to the ladies' room. Jackie had to pass her desk to get there and liked to stop and pick up the framed photographs of May's daughters, Laura on her veranda across the world, her face in the shadow of a palm leaf, Vera in fatigues and a lab coat, giving a shot to a thin man or woman—impossible to tell—draped in a Red Cross blanket.

The women have all heard stories of Vera and Laura, who have passed a kind of test in the office. Good daughters, both of them, however far away for the time being. The women have ascertained that letters come, and phone calls, from both girls, who are not girls by any means, but hardworking women in their forties. Vera calls from wherever she is without checking the time; she knows May welcomes a ringing phone at any hour of the night. She likes to settle in and talk to May, and seems not to care about who at her end will pay the bill. Often it seems to be a man, in some hotel where she has landed on leave for a day or two.

They know Laura is the tenderhearted one who writes books and, married to a doctor, can pay for her calls to her mother herself; Vera is the adventurer who could never get down on paper all she has to say about the night convoys and starved refugees, the filthy camps toured by diplomats, the exhausted teammates and talkative driver/spies and comrades and lovers who fill her days.

None of the women in the office, including May, would hesitate to ask questions or offer opinions—if not approving, at least deferring judgment—on the subject of each other's families. They know all about cruel in-laws and saintly ones, and spiteful siblings and no-contact orders and men who have to be forgiven. May has let the talk carry her away a few times. With their enthusiastic approval she has made reference to events in her own life. When she volunteered that she had had a lover but her husband never had, they weren't surprised at her but they didn't believe the part about her husband. When she said her friend Leah's divorce in the late fifties was the first divorce she had ever heard of other than among movie stars, they couldn't believe that either.

Most of them are young enough to have something to say about problem parents, and to have respectfully noted that May's, gone of course, were from a time when those raising families had fewer distractions and did a better job of it. "Another era," they said. "Simpler." May has countered with the information that things were not that simple; for one thing, a great number of people died young; her own mother did—something, they agreed, sadly characteristic of those days.

They know May had a son, as well as daughters. There is a small picture of him, too, in a silver frame on her desk, which they don't pick up and look at. They know she could not make a story of him. She always has a feeling Jackie is on the verge of picking the picture up, though; her hand seems to hover over it, almost in blessing.

Jackie likes to ask May questions about her daughters, or come around behind her—"Look at you!"—to tuck the label back under her collar, where the skin will go on ringing as if the pedal has been put down on a note.

In time, May began to keep a chair beside her for Jackie in the lunchroom, and liked to be the one to lend her money when they all ate out. Finally she fell under the compulsion of waiting for Jackie in the morning when she came in late, in a dew of apologies, shaking the static out of her pant legs, trailing her sadness, like Persephone let out of the depths.

"Heavens! Was that man there when you came in, in the garage, exposing himself?" says Persephone. Catcalls from the rest of the women. "You guys. Seriously, there ought to be some way he can get help. Well? Obviously he's in need."

The day of the flasher, May, like a real, established lover, was listening to a small unloving mockery of Jackie in her mind. This gave her some relief. But suddenly the doorway where Jackie was standing went dark as a negative. It grew veins like the sheen in coal. Her amusement was cut off by the fear, for the first time, that she really was having a stroke: fading room, vertigo, angel advancing to take her through that tunnel described in the near-death book.

If so it was a miniature, domesticated stroke, coming and going in three breaths.

If May doesn't leave the restaurant now she will be late for work. She gets up, she tips more than the cost of the coffee. *Old women don't tip.* It is hers, this nationality: *old women.* This country: *old.* Last night she planted her flag in it, in the middle of the night, hearing an echo in the room. Leg cramps awoke her. A beam of sunlight had been narrowing itself through the magnifying glass someone—her father!—held in his hand, until a tiny fire hissed on a dry leaf. Her legs hurt from crouching with him. She heard herself call someone to come.

She had a feeling she had shouted for her mother, she knew she had gone even farther back the second before she woke up all the way, and had been home from school in bed, her legs hurting. But she woke before the necessary moment, when her mother would be heard running up the stairs, hurrying to her, up from the cellar, her hands smelling of the potato bin—or no, how awful to have confused them—but it was deep night, May was barely awake—her potato-storing stepmother with her real, her darling mother, who would sit down on her bed smelling of type-writer ribbon and cigarettes and say, "How about a *story?*"

Of course it is May's own stories that draw Jackie to her desk, and often the others as well. They like to hear how May *gets around;* they squeal at what happens to her in ordinary places where they go themselves: restaurants, movie theaters, auto parts stores. They like her attitude.

Her story for today is about the boy who came and sat on the hood of her station wagon when she was stopped at a light. This massive, rust-eaten Ford that her daughters refuse to drive when they visit is hers because when she taught, she was the one who drove on field trips. Once it roared through the city with May at the wheel, to museums, parks, the Science Center, filled with the daydreams of teenagers packed thigh to thigh.

The boy climbed up on the bumper and rocked there, peering through the windshield at her before turning himself around on the heels of his hands and sitting down rather gently, considering he was on the hood. When the light changed, the car behind paused and then went around her. The driver was a woman, who pretended not to notice the boy sitting on May's car. May got out and said hello. She could never ignore a boy of this age, fifteen, sixteen. She said, "Anything I can do for you?" From the movies, she knows how to say that in a way somebody from the country of the young won't resent. She doesn't attempt their lingo but neither does she use conspicuous phrases from the past.

The boy looked down at his legs and up at the stoplight before he said, "Uh . . . ?" It came out a question, followed by a long pause. He was not going to be displaced, but he was swaying, hesitating. He was looking around for squad cars or the officers on bicycles they had now. If only I knew karate, May thought. She would have arced him lightly off the hood onto his back on the grass strip along the sidewalk. Then she would have invited him go to have coffee with her, if he drank coffee, and begin a new life.

That's what would happen in the movie of this encounter. The comedy. In the tragedy he would take the car. First he would have to shoot her. But no, the tragedy would be his life, not hers. If he shot her it would be accidentally; that would be in keeping with the trajectory of his existence. She would come late in the credits, having appeared for only those moments in the last scene: The Old Woman.

In her account it doesn't happen either way.

She asked the boy if he was sick. "Nah," he said. "I need a car." He was sizing her up, but she had the idea he couldn't see her very well, the morning sun behind her making him squint. "Aw, now," he said, "look like I could *have* this kind of a car."

"You ought to have a better car than this," May said. "You can see it has problems. You have to work your way into handling this kind of a car."

He made his hand a visor over his eyes and surveyed the block. "Aahhh . . ." he said, as if he might spit. "Keep it. I'm to the point . . . I'm done. I'm done. I can't get there anyway."

"Where?"

"Over to the center." He paused in thought. "My hours."

"Your hours. Community service? Juvenile court?" May said sharply. She knew about hours. They all said "my hours." The boy didn't answer, or even nod, he slid off the car and stood swaying. He paused to think, he grappled with desires in himself, she thought, that had no object. The things he wanted were not here, and could not be produced. He started away sideways, with his palms up, and when May followed, he ran. Now she was looking into the sun, and saw only his shape. He ran with grace and looseness, loose knees—she recognized this, this was heroin— his body dipping like a lighter flame before it comes to poise, but he managed it.

He ran away from her.

With her stiff legs, there was no question of chasing him to make him understand he had to get to his hours. All of his future, whether he would be permitted work, tenancy, fatherhood, even a life of any length, hinged on whether he could slide through a crack that had opened, whether he showed up, on this particular morning, where he was expected.

Don't disappear! she wanted to shout, seeing him pass straight out of some young social worker's patience, out of the folder marked Probation. Wait, don't disappear!

He didn't look back, either, to check if an old woman was in pursuit, clutching her chest.

When he shied against a Dumpster and rebounded into the alley and out of sight, May sat all the way down on the curb in her olive dress, dizzy and clammy. She hadn't had any breakfast. The restaurant with the skylight and the little girl were still ahead.

Don't tell that part.

Don't go on and on. Tell it briskly.

"Oh, May," Jackie would say with a sigh. "What if something had happened to you?"

"She was going to take him right on over to the center!" That would be Patricia. "She would do that."

"She *would*." Carmen, the supervisor, would fold her arms. "Wouldn't you? Admit it. You'd pick somebody up. You'd let 'em in your car. Oh, you have to be watched. We had better keep a very close eye on you."

Often they fell to talking about May as if she were a child. "I think it's those movies she goes to, don't you? She is running out to the movies. The R-rated, that's what she likes."

Sometimes at the office May feels like a child falling asleep in the back seat of a car, half hearing itself talked about, with everything left to others. Not with Patricia, who bullies her, but with the younger ones. She loses the sense of what they are saying, and feels

only the presence of them in their dry-cleaned blouses and perfume, with their watches, earrings, polished nails, their toes slipped
out of shoes, stretching against the nylon. No matter what might
await them when they ride down the seven floors in their coats to
leave the building, here inside, perfume hangs in the air and helpless laughter from the day before, from every day, waits to be resumed. These things are restful, like being rocked, or riding an
escalator that never arrives at the top, though it is going there,
where it seems something indeed might be waiting: a message, a
divine caress. Basking like this, she can await it.

The talk goes on until somebody looks at the clock and says,
"Well, I have a whole disk over there and if I don't do it today
Carmen will shit."

"I will," Carmen will say, disappearing into her own cubicle.
"I will do that, so get to work or I'll have you fired."

"I could sit here all day," Jackie will say, "but I guess I should
get something done. Everyone else is. Well, May. What a life. I
wish my grandmother took some interest in life, like you," as she
picks up her hair, in which bars of sunlight from the blinds are
lodged like combs, makes a tube of her fingers, and draws it all
smoothly down her back.

May is a year younger than Jackie's grandmother. If May were
a man, the gap would be less. Come to dinner with me, he would
feel free to say, because old age doesn't matter in men.

But that isn't true either. Two old men have apartments in
May's wing, the retirement wing. One is very old, and has a body
like a label that is peeling away; one day his hipbone will snap
dryly if he shifts as his foot comes down hard on the concrete
steps. Though fatigue covers him like ash, he dresses well; his suit
follows the caved-in lines of his body. He combs his yellow-white

hair with Alberto VO5, a smell May remembers. His son, who must be seventy, comes every day to take him somewhere. Son and father argue on the stairs over who is in charge of the descent.

The other old man has a stronger, denser body than the man in the suit. He has done work with it. He has lived in the building longer than May has, but his skin—she sometimes gets a look at him in the stairwell; like her he shuns the elevator—has not lost a certain sunburned tinge. Savage eyes, this man has, that flash at her as she comes up the stairs pulling on the rail, a message of hidden and secret, demonically persistent youth. Lately she has begun to feel a stirring of the same sort of feeling about him that she let herself in for when she started noticing Jackie. One little fire is not enough, apparently; another must sputter to life.

Still, she thinks, even if it conjures itself up out of nothing, love is not imaginary. If this feeling drawn out of her by the very sight of certain people is a kind of love. It's not the same thing as food eaten in dreams, of that she is stubbornly sure. The body feels it and it's real, it is always real.

Once she saw the man on his balcony as she was trying to ring somebody else in the building to let her in. It was early spring and unusually warm; she had left her coat at work with the keys in the pocket. The man's chin was turned to the sky, which was a rare March blue, streaked with the flame shapes of hurrying clouds, and he was grimacing, holding the railing as if he might rip it up out of the concrete. He did not belong in this building! It could not be he who lived in a building for old people, himself old! The blue and white sky streamed away from him. He looked down at May and she filled her hair out a little with her fingers as she looked up. *Oh, I'm weak in spring,* she thought, with a tenderness for her old habits. She took several backward steps to see him, backing into the little courtyard, which had a stone bench for them to catch their breath on. She felt for the bench behind her and sat down, not even checking to see if the pigeons had made a mess. She couldn't stop looking up at the figure on the balcony.

I'm in the same country, she wanted to yell up to him. She didn't ask him for help getting into the building, even though for a second she had imagined he must see the blue fire all around her.

Troublemakers: Nathanael

Troublemakers. Because of the home, and what was in it, because of the bad luck of being from a certain kind of home. "So you're a kid, and things are bad at home. You want to make trouble for somebody else, you want to get even. Anybody knows that who's missing a parent. Say a divorce. Say a parent dies."

May looks up.

"One parent is insufficient." The man has broken in on stories going around the table, a round table for eight with the napkins in cones on the dinner plates. She watches him.

They're in a hotel ballroom, behind a wall of draperies drawn across the spring night and bellying just a little where a rumor of the Chicago wind reaches them. They're talking about the classroom, about *troublemakers.* There is still just this category "troublemaker": no metal detectors, no blackened spoons in lockers, no despair. Or there must be despair. But no one says so here, no one at this education conference in 1960; they're talking about pranksters, fatherless misbehavers, motherless Huck Finns: *troublemakers*.

May has one or two in her classroom, one of them the author of a scrawled page in the pile she brought with her to grade in her hotel room, about a recent massacre in South Africa. She is surprised and pleased that this particular boy turned in anything at all, let alone knew of this event.

The headline on the newspapers in the lobby says, "U-2 Pilot Called Spy." At their table few believe the spy story. A social studies teacher from the South, a pretty woman in a sweater set May thinks would attract some notice in the classroom, complains to her, "You watch, the Kremlin is going to twist this. I told my husband, 'I don't care, you go down in the basement and fix us a shelter. We've got kids. We're too far out of town to get to the municipal building.'"

May believes the spy story. Obviously the plane was spying. The man she is listening to and watching believes it, she can tell. But before an argument can get under way, the whole table has swerved into whether Kennedy will take all the primaries, and then back to the matter of the school system.

He, a barrel-chested Negro man in his fifties, is principal of a small high school in the Midwest, the subject of an article they all have in their conference folders. May is one of a group of teachers receiving awards for their innovations. So many that it will seem, as they are called up to the stage by geographical region, that everybody in the smoky room is getting an award. The innovations are various classroom methods already in wide use, the real origins of which no one would be able to trace—they'll be laughing about that in the bar—methods that will go in and out of vogue two or three times over the years they are high school teachers.

For centerpieces the tables have little maypoles with rulers and compasses on the streamers, in support of the theme Math Closes the Gap. The gap is the missile gap.

Right after the election the missile gap ceased to exist, though for decades it didn't cease to hold certain jumpy children—May heard this from friends teaching grade school—in a spell of attention while a missile might or might not be glinting overhead, curving into its descent. May often thought of the missile gap rather bitterly, not for the reasons she might have expected of herself, political reasons, but because the words *missile gap* were part of that spring, with the sheaths and wide cloth belts droves of them wore up onto the stage to receive their engraved circle pins, the music—"Volare" in the piano lounge and in the elevator "Theme from *A Summer Place*"—and her first sight of the man she fell in love with in the eighteenth year of her marriage.

Somebody had taken the trouble to put together dozens of the maypole centerpieces for the banquet. "Those little rulers, can we take them with us for the supply closet?" "*May* we take them, *please*." This was the group cheerful and flushed from having escaped into the cocktail lounge before dinner, fleeing the lukewarm tea in the conference room.

The man she was staring at during dinner was not so jovial. He kept picking up his goblet of Hawaiian Punch and setting it down again. Not so many Negro faces in the crowded room. Four or five. He had the big knuckles of arthritis. Hands like that always caught her attention, a silent announcement of the body's presence as a *thing*.

There they were, hundreds of them in the room, bodies going about their own slow assimilating and shedding behind all the speeches and the voting, the slight but incessant activity of the meeting that they, the bodies, had to take part in, which had nothing really to do with them. Like the big carp with a tattered fin, swimming along the glass at the aquarium they had visited in the afternoon. In the wrong place.

It was just that body, that thing that nourished itself, swerved and dived, that May was to have in common with him. Lust—or so she thought for a long time. Excitement, cold and fresh. She thought she had drawn up a bucket with something in it, some element of herself on a simple errand of appetite; never did she think it *was* herself, or would become personal, grow limbs and make for land and for the occasions—embarrassing and frightening, grim, sweet, hazardous—of untimely love.

His hands were not restless, even tapping the glass with a fingernail that had a vertical dark streak in it.

The man looked at May too, at certain points in the conversation. An indulgence toward the others at their table flickered up between them. She saw him look at her dress and her in it. And then, as if by appointment, they met in the piano lounge. Women still eased themselves into bars in those days. You didn't just saunter in and order a drink, you pretended to be looking for somebody. That's what she did, she came down by herself after dinner, and there he was.

"Three times, we met after that. That's all we had. I wasn't the right type for a love affair, and I never did it again, I can tell you. It was a once-in-a-lifetime thing. He felt the same way."

May glanced back at her daughter, who had stopped on the sidewalk to laugh with her head thrown back. "Oh, God! Mom!

It's worse that you *smoked!*" Vera tucked May's arm against her. "Don't be offended. You aren't, are you? Go on. He felt the same way?"

Lovers came and went in Vera's life, men who were her friends, then not her friends, then her friends again if they were content to be. Men who were each other's friends, as often as not.

They were walking after dinner in an invisible rain. In the afternoon May had been to the eye doctor, and her dilated eyes were coming back to normal at a slower rate than the doctor had said they would. The streetlights and the neon signs wore soft, pliant auroras, making a slow, watery galaxy of the two blocks to the parking lot.

While Vera had read her the menu and tried out Spanish phrases on her, May had gone through a lot of the Chianti. Listening to Vera had filled May with an old, maternal pride and boredom. In the morning Vera would be leaving with another nurse-practitioner and two nuns for six months at a clinic in Guatemala. "Hope they don't arrest us. We've got a suitcase of narcotics. Made me think of Nick, when I packed the stuff."

Vera was like that. She did not fear the dead. She always walked right up to the subject of her brother and gave it a light, familiar, sisterly slap. You would not know she was the one in the family who had crouched on the grave before the stone was set in place, and battered the dirt with her fists.

In the dark restaurant May had had a hard time making out her daughter's face. Vera was the beauty of the family. May tried to focus on the dark eyes before her. Who would guess that behind the long lashes with their starry shadows lay a cockpit, all the switches on.

In the early part of the evening May had had herself in hand:

she would neither whine about Vera's departure nor start in on
the past, in an eagerness to prove to Vera that life had had the same
uprooting pull when she was Vera's age. A little younger, even.
Vera was forty-two. Unmarried. "Knowing my own nature," Vera
said, in the confiding always brought on by her leavetakings, "it
would be unfair to marry. I mean it. I can stand to be alone later."
Vera was not weak. She put her chin in the air. *Ah,* May thought,
*your grandmother did that very thing. The inch-long hair is all very
well, but it's the same chin, the same face. If you added freckles—my
mother's face.*

"I won't be alone, though," Vera continued, tearing off bread
and sopping up olive oil. "I'll have my friends." Women of her
generation gave friends the status once reserved for husbands
and family; they stuck together and would not let each other
down in old age. So Vera said. "So smile, Mom," she said, looking up.

Come, come, May would have replied, in her confident years.
You won't always be forty-two. Use your imagination.

The candle flame returned to a point because Vera's nail-
bitten, restless hands had finally stopped their gesturing and settled on the tablecloth. Once May would have picked one of them
up, breathed the olive oil and kissed the skin, no longer perfectly
smooth—but if there was a mark of her seventies it was that she
was altogether less sure of herself. Being with either of her
daughters now gave her the kind of shock you got in a foot that
had been asleep. Suddenly Vera was here, across the table from
her, unaged in spite of having cut her hair close to the scalp and
dyed it a darker, less becoming red, with the same obliviousness,
the stock of girlish energy intact, and here too, in May, was that
old unrest, that slow propeller stirring up maternal pride and

impatience while little sparks of torment leapt out of oblivion and faded back.

Friends, Vera had said. Not just family. Friends could feel all this, and stay bound together. For in friendship the element of pain was missing. *Is that it?* May thought. *And is pain the key element of love? And if not pain, then what?* That was when she plunged into the story of her love affair.

"Hold it." Vera snatched up the check. "I have to admit that I know this. I do, I know about this from Laura. She told me. I hope you don't mind. I don't see why you told her and not me." But she was yawning, she had to get on the plane in the morning ready to put on earphones and listen to Spanish sentences for many hours. "But go on," she said generously. "Tell me all of it. You told Laura, and I know she's the good sister, but now tell me."

Out on the wet sidewalk May took care not to stagger from the wine. "The funny thing was that the man was like me. He wasn't very set on accomplishing anything. Oh, he accomplished whatever they asked him to, he could do it. But he was a dreaming man. He had had parents like mine, doers, both of them—I mean he had grandparents. That's who raised him. Strong people. But he was always looking back. Whereas your father looked ahead. Your father was . . . my opposite in many ways."

"No shit," Vera said.

She didn't really have to worry, with Vera, as she had with Laura—Laura who studied what happened around her and had written a book about it, and followed it with another—about having to account for anything, any pain that might have been caused.

Vera frowned and said, "Wasn't the school boycott around then?"

May saw with a flash of rancor how her daughter would re-cast everything, making it into a political, *deliberate* thing. A thing forbidden in their day, and chosen because forbidden, that the two of them, May and her lover, had undertaken. Some *act,* on the order of the sit-ins that had begun around the same time. The way Vera always said, of her grandmother's fervent union-ism, "genteel." The way she had pointed out, in her SDS days, the roles cast for them all, middle-class people in the United States.

"This was before that," May said. "That was . . . I can't re-member." Memories had a way of excluding context, growing more and more concrete. The low-necked sheath dress, not the election, the song in the elevator, not the school system. The little maypoles, not the truth. Very little of the truth goes a long way.

For Vera's benefit she said, "When it started I thought it was physical. But as it turned out, he was a soul mate." That word of old. But even a word like that was no surprise to Vera, who said, "I've had that, with gay men. Watch it—curb. So hey! What was his name? Laura never told me."

"Nathanael." Now she had said it. Now the whole thing lay in wait, silent, mountainous, though such things were no longer mountainous, and Vera was hurrying her for the dates, the places, the moment of exposure, the outcome. May had a moment of horror at herself. "You know I would never have talked like this while your father was alive."

"I know."

Nathanael. "God has given," in Hebrew. Her best friend, Leah, had told her that.

Has given. In English, the perfect tense has a heartbroken sound. Is that right? I never taught my juniors that. Who could say they wouldn't have understood, some of them? Some of them had lives already frozen into the perfect tense, hardly room to move past seventeen or eighteen.

Like Nick, her own son.

Or the boy who wrote her the one page about the Sharpeville massacre, with his blunt pencil: "They go out next thing they dead."

Has given. A sound of wandering in an aftermath. I have come, you have forgotten, he has lost. God has given, and you, what have you done?

"And you, now, you're from Seattle," he said thoughtfully, with his head turned so he looked sideways at her. Seattle. That seemed to excuse her from history.

"Yes." She took a gulp of whiskey sour. He was drinking scotch and soda, setting it down on a small wet marble table that rocked on its base.

Why did you sit down with me? Of course he would not say that. It was important, though, to establish her innocence—not of history but of liberalism, of any off-center intentions where he was concerned, anything sexual, anything *racial*.

I sat down because of the way you looked at me at dinner, as if you knew me. Now you've turned the look off. But if I see it again, I'll know. What would she know?

His slightly bulging eyes met hers. His whole face was formed of swells marked off with grooves, like big kernels of corn, under the dark, freckled skin so taut it looked as if it might split open. A large, heavily molded face. His hair was silver at the edges. He was good-looking now, but what a handsome old man he would be. And she traveled years with him, right in front of him.

If he's doing the same thing he'll see a pasty old scarecrow, she thought. *Or maybe I'll be fat when I'm old, smoking by myself with my fat feet out in front of me. Or at the movies, buying popcorn. No, I won't be one of those old censors, I'll always go to the movies.*

Half the people in the bar were smoking, but something prevented May from lighting a cigarette in front of him. She wanted him to like her. The school where he was principal had been written up in the *Chicago Tribune* because it was the kind of school people wanted to read about. The article said his methods were a reassuring sign that the upheavals in education were going to stabilize. Though he didn't think so, he told May. Nothing was going to stabilize. Trouble was on the way.

Nathanael, his name was. He had a wife and family, all boys. How many boys? Though May knew that, she had the article. Six. Oh! One already twenty-two, three in their teens, two little ones. How old, the little ones? Three and one. Oh! "I mean, so many years of having them!" she said quickly. At that the rolled eyelids squinted a little. He put down his glass and threw his fingers out and down in a card-fanning gesture, rather an impatient, commanding gesture, catching her as she formed the ingratiating smile one offered at the mention of a stranger's family. *Stupid,* she said to herself. *Keep quiet.* Of course she had meant the pregnancies, six of them to go through over twenty years, not the surges between man and woman, not those, that spaced a family. A woman would have known what she meant.

Like the weight-guessers at carnivals, if you let yourself, you could receive a sort of wavering outline of a person's situation.

You could sense the movement of another life, shadowy figures, house, automobile, comings and goings with that illusory purpose of other lives. You could sense a burden. Kitchens, bedrooms in which faint voices made demands, promises. Six sons, each with a life to lift up and carry. Reproved, she sat back.

But the man had relented, he was chuckling. "My wife would agree with you." The cheeks pushed up firm creases around his eyes, in bunches like stems. Probably it was time to take her eyes off his face. The livid mark in the nail struck her as something he might have chosen to wear. She looked at it intently, feeling no peril.

It was her turn. She taught English, she had two daughters, nine and going on thirteen. Her husband was a doctor. Oh, a doctor. She flushed. She would not say, *But he wasn't always a doctor. He was poor, to begin with*. She did say, "It took him forever to finish his training because the war came." How long ago, that parting from Cole, and what a girl she had been. The whirlwind of mobilization stirring her despite her objections to war: truckloads of soldiers suddenly visible on the highways, warnings up and down the coast about fire balloons, the submarine that came out of nowhere and shelled Vancouver Island. The sight of Cole in his uniform. Thank God her mother did not live to see this war, a daughter's fingers on shining insignia, caressing. A girl daily offering the heavens her wild bargains for his safety.

"That's how I ended up teaching. I had wanted to . . ." Then she gave up. What had she wanted to do? It might be the look on the man's face was pity.

But in the next hour, submerged intuitions came to her and she recovered herself, made herself out a kindly-clever woman, in the scoop neckline of that year, a woman whose red dress and dark eyebrows might be seen to offset the blondish, fading hair and skin, and the silly pin they had fastened onto her dress at the banquet.

At last she made him laugh. When he laughed he didn't throw back his head as she had been doing, but bent it over his drink and rumbled as if he would permit himself just this level, curtailed amusement. She was describing her principal: her school was run by a theatrical woman, a fatedly stupid woman, whom May made funnier than she had ever thought her until that moment. He shifted in his chair; he was on his third drink, she her second. Her fingers and toes, her inner arms and thighs, had begun to hum.

Some bulk, some—girth, she told herself, looks good on a man. Yes, in middle age it gives off warmth. Cole shouldn't try to be so thin. She felt a stab of love for Cole. It was the hour when he would be sitting down at the piano to work the day out of his muscles, his skin red under the eyes where the surgical mask had been taped. Laura would be cooking his dinner, Vera stomping through the house with her ruined homework.

"Fallout," Nathanael was saying, in answer to some question she had dreamed up about his job. "I get the fallout."

"Fallout," she said, screwing up her face. They had all let a word pass in the blink of an eye from awful revelation to figure of speech. That was what she tried to tell her juniors. She could see on their faces the look that said they had been forewarned about her class. She would talk about the bomb, she would make them write a paper about atmospheric testing and dead sheep. It was too late: the real fallout had already blown into all of them, the world over. There were meetings about testing and May went to them, running off leaflets on the mimeograph machine in the school office, where that was seen as a harmless habit so long as you paid for the paper. But really she was just like everybody else, she kept at bay any thought of real fallout, a rain of poison from the sky, no shield from it.

She preferred sitting at the dining room table with her red pen, reading to Cole from her students' papers. *"The Ancient Romans invented the arch,"* she would read, as Cole ran his thumb up the keyboard. *"They let girls maried when they forteen."* Cole ran down the keys, struck a flat chord. *"But they beleved in slavery."* When the telephone rang both girls would jump up to get it, but it was always Leah. Leah, who taught math across the hall from May, was getting divorced. Hers was the first divorce in the school, the first involving anybody May knew. Nobody knew then what to expect, whether it was normal for a middle-aged teacher, even one with grown children, to get her ears pierced and begin reading Jung, and sell off the house and furniture that were hers by right.

Nathanael described his own school, to which the *Tribune* had sent a photographer to set up the shot that appeared in the paper over the caption "No-nonsense father of six raises six hundred." The picture had him at the lockers with a tough-looking kid in a T-shirt who had a bandaged hand. It was obvious, wasn't it? Was it? The kid was the son of a wealthy Jamaican lawyer. "A-plus student, first name *Holmes*. On his way to Brown."

May had fallen into a daze of friendliness. Her bare arm on the table felt graceful to her, her finger with its clear-polished nail slowly blending the condensation on the glass. She was filled with pleasure at the melting season outside the hotel, in the city of Chicago, where the spring wind sucked the draperies against the glass and corrugated the lake she had seen from the plane and again that afternoon at the aquarium. A bigger, more serious lake by far than the one at home, this one with a sea's dull roar, throwing spray high in the air as the women boarded their buses in the aquarium parking lot. They were teachers and the wives of teachers. The men at the conference didn't go on these sightseeing excursions.

May's feeling was that she had met no one in years for whom she felt such an immediate strong liking, if she ever had. From a certain sag in her movements she knew she had had too much to drink, but it was more than that. Sympathy welled up in her for everyone else in the hotel bar. *Oh, that woman can't stop talking,* she thought, at the sight of a gesturing woman with a double chin. *She just can't, and the man is tired of her, he's younger, the waiter is waiting for them to leave, waiting to get out of here to his real life, it's all so simple, so plain.*

In the middle of Nathanael's brown irises, around the pupils, floated uneven circles the color of gasoline. At a certain point she looked closely and felt them burn her.

Whatever it was, it had nothing tentative about it once it got going. It was the same for him, he told her later. Between them an unseen wire had begun conducting heat. They should have stepped clear of it and gone on their way. If they had had any experience, any caution, they might have risen casually from the table and said, "Well! This has been very nice." She could have held out her hand, at least to touch him once, and made some flattering admission such as "I've been enjoying myself a bit too much. Oh, if my students could see me! Obviously I can't sit in a bar half the night anymore." But it wasn't alcohol, it was the taut, invisible thread, unmentioned, growing warmer as they missed, one by one, the remarks that might have spared them.

He did drink. Drink was a carefully controlled area of difficulty for him, normally. He didn't mean to use that as an excuse,
he wasn't letting himself off the hook. No, he had been through
AA a time or two but it didn't stick, with him. He didn't drink *a
lot,* he never went crazy, the students never saw a sign of it.

He had a wonderful wife, a teacher. Last night, the first night
of the conference, he had drunk his first glass of scotch in six
months, at this same unsteady table. He did it because he was
away from his wife. It was his wife who kept things under control, held him steady. Of course tonight he was disgusted with
himself for having taken the drink, and that made it easier to
have another one. That was when May in her red dress had asked
if she could sit down.

Oh, so it was her doing? So women could just overpower
him, away from home?

Parts of his face seemed to swell. Quite suddenly you could
see the high school principal. "Never. You can believe that or dis-
believe it." She did believe it. Never before that time had this
man sat alone with a woman not his wife and given the silent,
frightening promise that had made itself felt between them.
"Until this, tonight," he added. He seemed to be leaning forward,
but he wasn't. *Whatever you say next,* she thought, *we'll do.*

In the morning she couldn't have said what they had talked
about in the bar. All the long evening at the table with him she
had been away, if she faced it squarely, away altogether. *On the
loose,* as Leah had said. Alert for the pause that went on a beat too
long, the look that should have cloaked itself immediately in talk
but did not, for his flat, almost tired, not-very-carefully-worded
suggestion when it came. Not even suggestion but acquiescence,
as if she were the one who had proposed it! When for all the

years of her marriage to Cole—*Cole,* her mind cried out faintly and sentimentally—even during her crushes, she had never even considered another man.

Nevertheless she was poised for it when it came. Poised as well for the sheathed casual trip past booths of teachers from the conference, her high heels sinking in the carpet. To the elevators and up, separately. His room, because he had no roommate.

She and Leah were sharing a room. The first afternoon, they had talked about what they would do if Leah should meet someone at the conference. A man. "The divorce is final," Leah had said. "I'm *on the loose.*"

"Twice is different from once," Leah said, the first time May ducked out of assembly to get her plane ticket to meet him. He had wanted to meet in Chicago, but already she had decided against going back to the same city. "You'd better give this a lot of thought," Leah said. "You're not unhappy, you and Cole."

It was true, they were not unhappy.

They had been, in the early days, when they were young and neither one of them knew what to do with the burden of jealousy and possessiveness leading to their exhausting quarrels and long-drawn-out reconciliations, or with their uncompromising expectations of each other, fierce and selfish. Somewhere underneath all of that were their reasons for stopping dead in the middle of perfectly good lives and marrying each other, as people all around them were doing with the war under way. These reasons, so vague and overmastering that May could never fully explain them even to herself, had braided themselves tightly over the years into that heavy rope of blind favor and routine opposition hardly movable, insensible of anything but its own fibers of pained tenderness, lying peacefully coiled in the sun. That was marriage. She and Cole were married.

So it was not true, the adage believed and repeated, endorsed in all the magazines, that a third person could not enter a marriage except through an existing crack. The truth was more insidious.

As for Nathanael, he seemed to want her but he did not. He wanted her, but not in life: in his imagination. Perhaps because he had lost his mother. That was Leah's interpretation. She had begun to see a psychiatrist, the first person of May's acquaintance to do this; she was reading Freud and Jung and dipping into *The Great Mother*. "And me—I'm the mother?" May laughed. "Are you kidding? The man has six sons."

She wanted no explanation. She wanted Leah to see what had happened in all its sudden, forbidden, irresistible worthiness. Its inevitability. Yes, she wanted Leah to submit to it, as she had submitted.

Leah said not to pull everything down around her just because at forty she had succumbed to a momentary attraction. Leah was older, in her fifties. "The man's my age!" Leah said. "I could tell him a thing or two." Leah might be divorced now, but she had been very careful not to let things go when her own children were young.

When they met the second time, Nathanael took a picture out of his wallet and showed it to her. "I'm sorry, it's not funny," she said, laughing, "but your mother, really, she looks a little bit like my stepmother. No, I mean it." For this was a calm girl with a circlet of braids, showing the camera a broad, sweet, low-slung face with something willful in it.

His mother had come to Ohio from Alabama, early in the century, and found work in the hotel where his father worked. They were twenty when they married.

This was the conversation she shouldn't have related to Leah, who, even before the psychiatrist, had gone in for what she called "solving for x."

"May I look at the rest?"

"If you like."

There were his sons, his smiling wife, not heavy and confident and stylish as May had pictured her, but lean, big-eyed.

"Here," she had said, taking out her own wallet, where she kept so many pictures the thing fell open like a fan. Cole, the girls, her students, friends. "See, there's my stepmother. The braids. See the resemblance?"

"Can't say I do." He studied every picture, without comment, and gave her a long look when he handed back the wallet, one of the looks that rested her inexplicably. They were in a hotel restaurant, in a high curved booth where they could sit pressed close.

"All those people." When he made no reply she said, "Tell me about her." The picture of his mother still lay on the table.

She knew his mother had died. As he spoke May could see it in his broad face as if it had just happened to him. She had died when he was five years old. It must have been that, not the wife and sons, that she had glimpsed that night at the banquet table, and again in the bar.

"You must have had a stepmother?" But he had not. His father had been one of those widowers who don't make a second try. That was the pattern in his family. Except for one happy woman, the grandmother freed from slavery in her teens, who rejoiced and sang and prayed the day long—with that one exception, it appeared, Nathanael's family was ruled by silence, self-reproach, and bullheadedness, coming down through generations. There was a religious streak. The women fell out in church, the men worked fanatically hard and inched ahead. If someone died they never got over it. His grandfather had suffered losses enough that he did not open his mouth to speak more than once or twice a day, though it was he who had married the talkative, happy one who had been freed in her girlhood. When Nathanael's mother died, his father took him over to the grandparents' house with his clothes and coat and shoes in a Sears, Roebuck box, and his one book, the Bible, and his grandparents raised him.

"He really did that. And you were five. Well, I guess I can't complain that my father remarried the year my mother died."

"A lot of folks will do that. Don't forget this was 1913." By then she knew his age, fifty-two; she knew many things about him not unfolded to anyone since his wedding day. His wedding *night,* when he and his wife had first let down their guard. That was not so unusual then, he said, to wait a while before you told on yourself.

"Don't. Don't make me think about her. Are you? Are you thinking about her? But your father, in 1913—back then men got married as fast as the women could die off, didn't they?"

"Not in my family." He threw his heavy arm around her, his mouth pulled childishly downward.

"To tell the truth, I never got over it, that my dad did that," May said. "That he brought somebody straight home. I don't think I ever forgave him." The truth was not so simple; she had loved her stepmother. Yet that was the start of an evening in which she set before Nathanael, and even heightened, the drenching sorrows of her teens, as well as certain buried cravings of the present time. Not those too minor to be known to her until gratified, such as the wish to have hands enclose her face, as Nathanael's had already done through his own inclination more than once, with their big arthritic fingers and their palms like warmed cushions. But secret things, things too perverse or long-standing to bring up so late with Cole, in the established rhythm of a household.

In a more temperate way, Nathanael had been doing the same, scratching his close curls and wondering at so much he had forgotten about himself.

"Well now, May," he said, at length. Then because of her name on his lips, and because the atmosphere seemed changed, as if they had cleared up the subject, they relaxed, a cleansing energy flowed through them, they smiled at each other with an absurd happiness and in their room returned to the kissing, the hungry, hopeless breathing of sighs, the lying down, the loss of themselves.

"So Mom, don't take offense," Vera said in her practical way. "But now, what were you to him? I mean, looks, of course—I remember wanting to look like you. Wait, I'm not saying it was that. But did he know you? Did he know my mom? How old was I?"

"You were nine."

"Did I ever see him?"

"No, no one saw him but me."

"OK, so he was wild about you?"

"I think he was. I can't say why."

"I'm serious, did he want you to get divorced? Don't fall."

May had put one foot off the curb. "I don't think he ever did. I don't think so."

"I'm being a shit," Vera said. "You don't have to tell me."

"But I think if he had asked me to, I would have been in a mess. I might have tried to. Before Nick was born."

They were getting close to the part Vera did remember. With her own stories, Vera would tell anything, go anywhere. But she stopped May there, in her story. She helped her into the car. She told her to close her eyes and not look at the headlights.

Her will had deserted her. Her will, except for that part of it she had to exercise to get to him, had nothing to do with what took place between them. So for a time she was quiet. It seemed to her that anything she said or did might surprise or offend him, or hurt him. She couldn't fight with him, or exult in his subjection to her when it came, because by then she was not fit for power.

After those hours of staring at his face the first night, she was embarrassed sometimes to look at him. When she first saw him the next time, coming toward her in the airport, she had to turn her head to avoid his big eyes on her with their pressing, exposing knowledge.

In her life with Cole, a staring down, a regular tipping of the balance went on, making it possible for them to establish themselves again and again, or force a pause, a change of course. If that was a contest, as Vera was fond of saying it was, it was not a bitter one. There was energy in it, there was a comical, invigorating repetitiveness. But with Nathanael she was at rest. And he, too, with his strong, practical wife and her ideals and efforts that carried the big family along toward some culmination that was, he confessed, a mystery to him: with May he was at rest. He told her so the second time they met, and she felt it in his own lapse into silence, from one meeting to the next, and in his hands, and the weight of his head on her chest.

Could she be blamed for allowing the thought to form, in those months, that there must be meaning in this, that their households, their schools, and the ten unsuspecting hearts that cruelly hindered them might have to be broken in on to make way for it, that a child might already have come of it?

Yes, she could be blamed.

All May could have said about the weeks after the baby was born was that they were running on, while she had stopped. She felt them skimming under her when her eyes opened on the sight of Cole and the girls in the room where she had lain all day passing fitfully in and out of sleep, with the baby beside her in the smelly bed, asleep in his wet diaper, with his swollen navel and a crust on the tiny flat gills that were his nostrils. A helpless newborn an arm's length away, all that time. Awful. Her own child Vera had the sense to be outraged. Laura did not have time for outrage; she just took over. Laura was the pharaoh's daughter; she dragged the basket out of the bulrushes and picked up the baby.

Snow was falling. She could see it from the bed, endlessly passing the window as if the house were rising.

"Thank God someone in this house is sane." That was what

Seven Loves

Cole said to May, in furious despair. May could have been in the basket herself; she could feel the slosh under her. She felt a little of the ebbed-out life run back, remembering the word *bulrushes,* a word she had loved as a child. "I'm sorry. I'm sorry," she kept telling Cole.

During the day, when the girls were in school, Leah came over on her lunch hour to check on the baby. "When did you change him? Oh, look at his bottom all sore, isn't him? Oh, the poor little man. Yes! You yell at your mommy. Oh, May."

Later May said, "Leah, this isn't me. Is it?" They were both looking into the bedroom mirror, at her in her bathrobe, with puffy eyes and lines around her mouth.

"It had better not be."

Once every week or so, when the girls came in from school and took over, she put on her clothes; she went down the steps into the garage and started the car and drove to Leah's house. Yes, she could be trusted at the wheel of a car. But there was snow on the streets. That was all right, she was a different person in the car; she had always been the one to drive, wherever they went as a family. No, she wouldn't run over anybody.

Leah always opened the door to her, hugged her. Why did she do this? Why not say, *Shape up or you're no friend of mine.*

"I won't go on like this, I'll get over it," she told Leah firmly. Just saying it, she was getting over it. It was a question of throwing off the wish to lie still and moan.

Leah liked to bundle up a life and push it off in a boat. The boat belonged to you, had been yours from birth. You might as well sit down, you were in it already. That was only your shadow on shore debating whether to go. As well debate whether to digest your food. She wouldn't let May smoke in her presence anymore because that was part of the negating, the *death-seeking* in May. For the first time in weeks May laughed out loud, in Leah's kitchen where she had dragged herself. *Death-seeking*. In her! who was *married* to life.

"I don't like explanations of life and I never have," May said one day, and that was how she knew, with relief, that she was getting back her opinions.

"We didn't know," Leah would say when they looked back on that time. "There was no reason for you to know, but I should have." Even Leah, with her Jung and her magazines and her psychiatrist, had been surprised to find that the condition May was in after the baby's birth had had a name.

Nathanael left education and entered a second life as a politician, of all things. Drafted to be mayor of his little city in the Midwest, he stayed in office for years. He stayed married, as May did. Every year they wrote a few words at Christmas. All six of Nathanael's sons did well, the two older ones very well. One went to Washington; you could see his name in the papers. Nathanael was twelve years older than May; he was getting old, becoming, two thousand miles away, the handsome old man who had flashed into her mind in the hotel bar.

But not before they had their occasions. For the last of these she had invented a meeting. "Another one?" That was Cole. "The teachers are out-meeting the doctors."

"I don't want to do this, May," Nathanael said, the third time. "I'm drinking, at home. I don't want to drink."

"I'm a sinner," she said bitterly.

"Sinful girl," he said, without smiling. "I'm too old. I could almost be your daddy. That makes me responsible. I'll get away from you."

"Get away from me," she said, pulling him against her.

Finally he said, "No, May. This is it. No more. I've been in torment. I've been sitting up in the church. I've been down on my knees." They were in the train station. He spoke slowly, while May ground her head into his shoulder. She was pregnant; he had his hand on her belly with the child in it. "I call myself a Christian!" He spoke as if May, allied with her own body against him, would be at a loss to know what he meant by the term. By then, though, she did know. She knew she had been flattering herself, making the mistake of thinking he must see that he was like her: marked, motherless. *Hers*. A man like him, a Christian.

In the train station she went over what he had said about sitting in the church in torment.

Torment. Away from him there was not as much torment in it as she would have expected of herself. No more than if she had been in an accident and had to be knocked out for the time it would take to recover. Away from him, waking and sleeping, her mind persisted in childishly dwelling on her own sensations. A constant low vibration of excitement left her standing in the supply room some afternoons with her cold hands on the chalk and pencils and her forehead against a shelf.

The first time, there had been only the surrender to unthinking, unnerving pleasure, and afterward their first taste of the comfort they would be to each other in what seemed to be a form of friendship, a shamed friendship.

By the third time, she drank in the bar with him and speculated giddily about a full confession to both families and a step off into the thin air of a life somewhere in the world where they might possibly live. "You don't mean that," he said with a forbidding calm.

He had come all the way to Seattle; Cole was away and Leah had the girls for the weekend. His window looked out on the Sound, and in the afternoon seagulls dropped to the ledge and sat with blowing feathers. "Spies," she said, and drew the curtains, but he wouldn't joke; he never would. And the hotel room in the same city with her own house seemed to warn her, with its wrapped soaps and maps and directories, that it existed for someone not herself. Going down to the bar with him she prepared herself for the stares. This night drew to a close in protracted tears that left her with a sore throat. Following that, she narrowed down to asking for one more day in the hotel, and finally merely for a promise that he would call. She had always been the one to call. He could, he must, call her at school. She kept repeating it. Behind the mimeograph was a phone where the teachers could take a call in private.

When they met for the last time she built up to a hopeless wrath and ran to lock herself in the bathroom, where after half an hour she fell to putting on makeup with no embarrassment and calling to him to unpack her new nightgown and hand it through the door. In the morning she watched him move slowly around the room in his brown skin and white shorts, eyelids swollen, heavy mouth in a frown. When he sat down and faced her she shut out his voice and kept her mind on the two colors in his irises, the deep creases in his forehead.

It seemed to her she had never seen a man before in the way she was seeing him, never realized what a man was, how concealed, while exposed to any insult. How comically bound to show himself as both strong and harmless, to shave his jaws smooth and hide his big shoulders and belly, his whole greedy, wary, delicately sensing body, in a suit. His wife bought his suits. They were nicer than anything Cole had in his closet. His wife left them on layaway for months, making the payments.

This time he had flown to Portland. Where had the money come from for his ticket? After he left, she sat by herself in the train station, leaning on the tall wooden back of the bench. It was like a pew. Where exactly did he get down on his knees? Was it in church or in his house? What if the three-year-old ran in? Or would he be used to the sight of his father on his knees? She had been sitting on the bench as if thrown there; she should cross her legs. Her body felt as if she had been in a bathtub too long. It felt scalded. Four hours ahead of her on the train, for grading papers. She shut away the shocked face of the maid who had come into his room, and the stark lies involved in two phone calls to Cole, and the word *love* formed with lips crushed against skin. When she took off her coat in the hotel lobby the people who had been watching them had seemed reassured: she was pregnant. What could that have to do with the two of them? They must be officials of some kind. He must be foreign. A dignitary, in that suit. Of course. That kind of dignity, in a man like that, would be foreign.

She could imagine the arranging of possibilities that excused them, the relief.

On the train she held the test papers in her lap but her eyes closed and she slept through the miles. She dreamed she was on a train with a man she didn't know, and had inadvertently begun kissing and caressing him. She knew something was amiss about it but she couldn't stop. The heat of the situation was tangled up with some feeling of herself as a child, when pure joy could attack you out of nowhere and force you to leap and run. But she couldn't be a child, because of what she was going to do. No, she was grown, she was free to do this, she must do it. But the dream ended before they could find a place to lie down.

When she saw Cole she trembled. She thought, for the first time, *There's something the matter with me.*

Was this torment? For he, Nathanael, had been on his knees. This should not have surprised her but it did, making her wonder about the other surprises, given time, and a different world, given everything that was not given, the injuries and avowals, the sinking into pleasure and union and grief, the marriage that might have been theirs.

The baby was Nick. Her last-born.

In summer she knew the time for resolve, the time for the truth was at hand; she put it off. School started. Daily, nightly, hourly she went over it, in bed at night, in the shower, in the car, in the teachers' lounge gobbling potato chips, in class while heads were bent over the tests she had passed out and the smell of mimeograph ink on her hands was making her sick. At first it was just fog. Her mind sent low beams out into the fog and found nothing by which she could orient herself in order to make a decision.

First she thought, *I'll wait, Cole will see when the baby is born, he'll see. He'll know, it will be taken out of my hands.* But what cowardice, to hold off, to wait that way to be exposed. No, she couldn't wait, she would have to tell Cole. The affair was over.

She would start with that. There would be no mention of how boldly she had begun it, how knowingly waded out beyond her depth.

And if the baby was Nathanael's, as she believed, what did she think would happen to all of them when it was born? Nathanael had broken with her. Did she think he would see it and change his mind? And Cole—did she think Cole would leave her, leave his daughters? Or take them from her? Was that what she wanted to do to her family?

Cole was strong. His confidence was a kind of muscle; it could repel a blow. She thought so then. And she was strong; she was going to start in on this baby's life, on the practical arrangements—her leave from school, crib down from the attic, cardboard box of the little undershirts with snaps—for this third, late child.

She had told Cole so many times in her mind that when she got started she was hardly aware she was really telling him. And then she didn't do it—watching his face she fell back, she didn't say *lover.* With elbows bearing down so hard on the table her arms and ribs ached by the time she stopped talking, she told him part of it.

I went to bed with a man, she said. She said *at a conference,* and let it stand, the implied *once.*

About the baby—suddenly motionless inside her as if listening—she said nothing. And neither did Cole. If it occurred to him to work out the dates, he gave no sign. This omission was almost worse than the rage she had feared. Rage would have been a sign of a certain objectivity.

Cole's lips were white; he could not complete a sentence or meet her eyes. "In that case . . ." he said several times, going no further, as if she were laying out a theorem to which he could supply only the little deltas, the *therefores*. He was rubbing grains of sugar into the kitchen table with his thumb as if he could rub out the grain of the maple.

May was saying *a man*. She never spoke a name, never said *love*. Her skin felt starched. She had stumbled into this dignified way of talking and could not break out of it. *This* is *me,* she thought. *I am this awful, troublemaking, greedy woman who makes up a ridiculous lie.* All she was explaining to Cole seemed to refer to long ago. She had stopped fearing he would say, *When?* It was not good to be as free as he was leaving her, to despair of punishment. The girls were out; the house was quiet. All around them was a silence, ready to come forward and cover everything she had said. She made the silence an offering: no detail, no painful description would pass her lips, nothing more to hurt him. But he didn't ask.

You must be this way in the operating room, she thought, suddenly angry. No questions, just the thing at hand, just the slimy red flinching heart. But then she thought, *All right, you have to be. That's all right. Heaven help me if I make this your fault.* She didn't say she had smoothed the skirt of her red dress and walked in hypnotized celebration to an elevator, and after that gone shamelessly up to the desks of hotels alone, and *seized hold* of a man Cole had never seen, a man she loved.

It was then that Cole said, "It's his baby, isn't it."

"It's possible," she said.

Would that have been the right thing to do, tell the rest of it, the whole truth? The truth. If you packed it down the mass was still there. The chemical effect. If the effect of a little piece of the truth was as bad as that—the pinched lips, the face gone pale as his hair, eyes drained of blue, half shut as if she were waving something too close to them—what would more of it have done? What would more of it do, when the baby was brought to him, kicking its little dusky legs?

But the baby that was born was not Nathanael's child. He was Cole's.

His small square head was covered with the unmistakable flax. He had the little basking furrow from nose to upper lip that was Cole's, and Cole's defect, the little crimp in the crest of the ear. His eyes were the peerless fjord-blue.

May looked into them, searching for what she had always felt with her babies, that slow dive of rapture. The baby. *I will have to love him. I will have to get over it. I promised.* She turned to the wall.

If only she hadn't said that. That spell. She had drawn her own blood. If only she hadn't said, *I'll have to love him.*

The baby was jaundiced and she stayed with him in the hospital for ten days. That was what you did then. A social worker came to sit at her bedside before they let her take him home. "It will all come back to you," the woman said, as if May had amnesia. "Normal feeling will return."

May said nothing about the affair, but the woman treated May as if she had something to hide, of which she could rid herself if she buckled down.

The affair was over before she ever beheld her newborn. Nathanael had put a stop to it. She had destroyed his letters but she had the final one with her in the hospital, in her purse. He meant what he had said in that letter. He had prayed about it. He would take responsibility for whatever happened when the baby was born, and he would come to see Cole and bow his head and ask forgiveness. But he had had his fill of that life where someone is missing. He'd had the life of an absence; he wouldn't bequeath it to his two sons still at home, the little ones.

It was not secrecy or adultery that had decided him. Not the urgent, shamed messages in code that traveled from his school to hers. It was himself, a boy without parents.

A faint thrill went through her at the thought of his big face clenched in prayer, with her as its subject. How strange, how unknown to her he was, when she had said to herself so many times, *I know him. I don't care how unlikely it is. If I had met him first, when I was twenty, I would have known. He would have known.*

She had written it in letters and said it aloud, and she was glad of that. But she was glad too that she had not done more, flown to his city, or begged any more than she had. She was glad her will had been diluted, and so little had been planned for in the way of a future for such meetings. Almost nothing. They had hardly begun. Yet the weight of him was on her, she could not move him, or remember what she had thought about before she thought about his sternness. His absorption in the church. His having had no mother. His nail with the mark, his hands, his carved eyelids, his full, gloomy face coming down to hers.

May did know, in time, that at a later date little of what had happened to her and to her baby would have taken place. A drug would have been provided. The disturbed mother would not have cried at the sight of her baby being brought to nurse, and lost her milk and cried on thinly for weeks with the child crying beside her, instead of in her arms. Because—and she could not stop recalling this, wondering if she remembered it accurately— she had not held the baby. Not very much. She had kept him in the bed with her, not in his crib, but Laura, smelling of food, drying her hands and pushing up her wet sleeves, had come and scooped him up at all hours of the day, and walked up and down the room with him, murmuring and cooing, with her oily bangs falling over the thin curled fists he held up in front of his face as if he were still in the stage of petitioning to be born, still floating, anchored.

"Laura, honey, take a bath, wash your hair," May said weakly.

"I will," Laura said, laying her cheek passionately on the baby as if she could absorb him.

"*You* wash *yours.*" It was Vera, the shadow at the door. She was speaking to May.

Until he got pneumonia, the baby mostly slept while May did. Drugs for depression were different then; there were no drugs then at all, really, in normal life, the way there would be in a few years.

Nothing that was coming was dreamed of. There were no essays being turned in at school, in a child's handwriting, about nightmare drug trips. No hash, no windowpane. No pills, no angel dust.

Or none that you heard of, saw, touched in wonder when you entered the kind of filthy room that someone—in a very few years there were people who would do this—would rent to a fifteen-year-old kid, a runaway, so that he could sell himself to buy drugs.

No hallucinating sons trying to get in, at the back door in the rain, screaming, "The deck, no, no, look, the deck, it's covered with snot!" while flashlights played from upstairs windows where the parents, figures in pajamas, old as ghosts, could be seen crouching in the dark.

Nick was born in 1961. All that was to figure in his life had barely been born itself.

Nick was not going to die, as May had feared when he was born small, in the first percentile, and "icteric," as the chart said. Cole was allowed to read it because he was a doctor, and May read it over his shoulder. In those days you didn't ask to see a chart, you didn't come out with the words she had been repeating to herself in a weak snarl, "It's my baby, what have you written about him?"

She had had a C-section. She had labored and labored, until she heard the resident say, "He's holed up in there and we're going to have to go get him. Or her."

She knew it was a boy. In comparison the girls had come with a friendly ease. This had nothing easy about it.

The yellow of the baby's skin faded under the bilirubin lights, he gained a few ounces, and they allowed her to take him home. "I don't think I can drive," she said foolishly.

"No one expects you to drive," said Cole's voice.

In the car she cried and apologized for it, whispering, "What did they give me?"

She meant drugs, but Cole said harshly, "They gave you your baby." Through half-closed eyes May inspected the blond, tiny, floppy male thing that was her baby. The skin around his eyes where the eye patches had been taped was like chewed gum.

At home, in Laura's hands, the baby gained four ounces.

When Cole came in at the end of the day Laura would place the baby in his arms, bring the bottle, arrange a diaper over Cole's shoulder. But Cole didn't like to put the baby to his shoulder, he liked to look him straight in the eye, roll the tiny fists in circles. He liked to sing to him. He produced a quavering falsetto. He would sit in the rocking chair May had used when both girls were babies and sing "Home on the Range," and "Down in the Valley." *Give my heart ease, love, give my heart ease / Throw your arms round me, give my heart ease.* May knew that song, and *Oh! I long for Jeanie and my heart bows low / Never more to find her where the bright waters flow.* She tried to open her eyes, to smile. Through a fog she could hear Cole, see him rocking. But who was he to her?

The baby got pneumonia. He had a convulsion; he lay in the hospital with his bowlegs sticking out of a little tent. But he was not going to die of pneumonia; he was not going to die for years and years.

"It's all right," May said. She was in the chair, resting her forehead on the bars of the aluminum crib. "Never mind."

"Was it real gold?" Vera said, biting her lips.

They were talking about May's locket, which Vera had lost. All three of them were gowned but not masked, because no one had told them to put on masks. That would make Cole so angry he would go out to the nurses' station and call the head of pediatrics. He had the floor, the department, the whole building hopping for this son of his. There was a hush of sympathy among the nurses who had teased him when the girls were born, long ago, in another life; there was a narrowing of the eyes whenever May—

they had teased May too, both times before—cried or came weaving to the door of the baby's room and peered down the hall.

"Who cares if it was gold?" Laura said sharply.

"It's all right. It was one of those necklaces they had in the mercantile back then, three or four of them hanging on a cardboard at the cash register. My sister got it for me, for my birthday."

"But it had your mother's picture in it," Laura persisted.

Your mother. Grandma, to them, was her father's second wife. May had never really believed they did not know the person she was talking about when she talked about her mother. My mother *died,* she had sometimes specified, to threaten the knowledge into them.

"It did have her picture in it."

"What made you think you got to wear it?" Laura demanded. "You just went in their room and took it."

"Oh, Mom, oh—" Vera jumped up, knocking over the folding chair the nurse had brought in. Laura picked it up while Vera paced up and down the room with her arms crossed, holding herself by the little biceps and shaking her head. Vera was ten. She was not so much a dramatizer as a child who claimed things, people, occasions for herself. "Oh, I don't know what could've happened! Honestly!"

"It's all right. Believe me, honey. It is."

"Oh, Mom." Vera gave a sob. "I just went in your room so I could open it and look at the picture."

"Why don't you shut up?" Laura said. "Really, Mom, can't you make her? You're the one whose locket is gone, and she's howling. She wore it to softball!"

"We went all over the diamond! We crawled around. We *looked!*"

"Oh *yeah.* I'm so sick of it, I'm *sick* of it." Laura had flushed almost purple—calm Laura. "I've had it with her. The baby's so sick. She can't be the center of everything that ever happens." Laura shut her eyes. Then her voice lifted up in a moan, a strange, high, barking whine. "I hate her. The baby's so sick. I know he'll die!" She turned to May. "I hate you too! I hate *you!* You don't even care!"

It was then that Cole arrived. Laura sagged against the metal cart with the baby bottles. "Daddy," she sighed, as if an elevator falling with her in it had set down softly.

Cole had been in the operating room; his damp blond hair was marked by the strings of the mask that hung around his neck. The minute he came in he wheeled around and went out again, and they heard his voice raised at the nurses' station. When he came back he had fresh, pressed masks for all four of them to put over their faces.

He bent over the crib. At first May thought some fluid was springing out of the papery skin the baby had, discs of moisture squeezing out. Then she saw it was tears, dropping from Cole's eyes. A sob broke from him. She heard a spring in the side of the crib give under his weight. She saw his head hanging over the baby's legs, and felt a slow, spreading shock as she stared.

She remembered Cole. She remembered him. It was the breakthrough of normal feeling the social worker had spoken of, the expected, the awaited relief. Cole. Poor Cole. The mask was sucked into his open mouth so that he looked like a mummy. She followed his gaze down to the baby.

Nicholas. They had all four chosen the name. Victory, it meant. Laura had bought a book of baby names.

Both girls bent over their brother. Nicholas.

A nurse said, from far away, "His penicillin." His. Already the baby had things that were his. His IV. The nurse was working a needle into the IV line. A bigger needle was taped to his scalp, where the good veins were in babies, Cole said. All around the tape the skin was pulled and wrinkled. One of his eyes was crusty; he had scratched his cornea with a fingernail. His. His tiny fingernails, just cut. Hours ago May had seen the shreds fall as the nurse cut them. "Nobody fixed these little bitty nails for you, did they?"

"So you thought you might open those blue eyes for a minute, huh?" This was the same nurse. With a little frown at May she said, "Your son sure can sleep."

Your son. *Of course he can. Of course he sleeps. He's sick and he's afraid.*

My son.

His blue eyes were open, roving, though his fingers lay passively curled. That was when the truth gave off a little of its chemical heat. *My son.* That was when the scalding began, that pain that will sometimes set off the fiercest indulgence, the wildest preference—the pouring down inside her scalp and shoulders and breasts, the scouring of her belly to its floor, the love for the baby Nicholas, the curse of love she had laid on herself.

THREE

Olga Sobol: Cole

long the highway following the river north the sun came out and they could see eagles sitting in the bare branches. The leaves were new, still a green film on bark. May counted nine eagles before her eyes fell shut.

"Black Acre," read a crude sign with an arrow, when she opened them again. And at the next farm, "Pressure washing. Moss removal. Rabbits." The sun had withdrawn. Her drowsing mind surveyed the few cars being drawn along the road with them, each with its toy figures inside, into a still landscape of ploughed fields, house trailers spellbound in fog, and flocks of wet sheep. The fog lifted on a sudden acre of llamas, grazing in the mud under thin rain and their own rainbow. At that house there were a dozen cats on the porch and more scattered in the little field with the llamas, watching the grass. Stretching, May pointed them out to Cole. "I thought cats hated the rain."

"These cats are half wild," said Cole, who had never been in the area before and had no special knowledge of animals.

At the hospital Cole decided very quickly what something was and what to do about it. He had to. All surgeons did this, he claimed; they all decided in this way. Pronounced, May said. If so, he said, that was what was required of them.

"Uh oh, she'll never let you get away with that," her friend Leah used to say when he came out with one of his assertions. And now May had to wait for them, even solicit them, so the valve would open to let in a quick, hot jet of his old pride in himself. His old lordly certainty—how could she have tried to break him of it?

By the time they crossed into Canada the rain had stopped and the sun was out. From his booth the customs agent looked into the car without interest, though with a certain weary probity. May felt his glance pass over her, full of knowledge of the things people tried to get away with. His gray face—how did the old shave those seams and moles?—and red-rimmed eyes. This would be a good job for an old person who had to have a job. A widower whose apartment was stale with a lone man's neatness. His fingers were the color of cement, and as he questioned Cole, one of them absently, tenderly rubbed the furrow beside his mouth. May leaned forward in her seatbelt and met his eyes.

A bolt of something in the eyes—of being a man in a booth, old, on a quiet border—traveled into her. It took her breath away. To dispel the feeling, when he had nodded them through she said lightly, "You know, I'm turning into one of those people who get messages in their fillings." Cole didn't answer. Since his heart attack he had trouble paying attention. "All of a sudden," she persisted, "I'll get a message. I got one just now. Why would I keep having this feeling of . . . I don't know what?"

But when she turned to look at the old man she saw that for

the blond girl at the wheel of the next car he had shed his tragic calm and produced a grin and a jaunty wave. She sat back, her startled relief complicated by a need to pull down the visor and look at herself in the mirror.

"It's a mystery to me," Cole said, without asking what message she might have received. He pointed at a sign. "Twenty-five kilometers. Are you awake? This time can you tell me before the exit?"

"You think it's my age." She was fifty-five. "But maybe I'm supposed to do something."

"You're doing something, you're teaching. Plus keeping track of Nick. A full-time job."

"I don't mean that, I don't mean my job, I mean . . ."

"You mean maybe you're supposed to get through to the president?"

"Maybe I am. It could be I have secret information."

He still went with her to spy movies and thrillers. And he would sit through a comedy, and laugh, in places. He wouldn't watch anything serious now. No "drama." Not long after his bypass she got hold of a questionnaire, "How's Your Mood? Ten Character Basics," in a magazine her students were passing around. These surveys were in all the magazines because it was the year of the mood ring. The high school girls joked about the rings but it was true that they were freshly conscious of their own natures, registering in color from the heat of skin. May showed the questionnaire to her friend Leah and they filled it out on Cole. A low score indicated optimism; Cole's, in Leah's firm tally, was close to the highest. Laughing in movies had saved him two points.

"This puts him in greenish-gray," Leah said, describing the

result to May's daughter Vera. "Mud color. That's bad. And he—
you know him, he thinks he's fooling everybody. Hey, I bet you
have a mood ring on you."

"I do not! And I think it goes all the way to black."

Vera was on leave from the hospital ship that had been her
home for a year. She had arrived in tinted glasses, a leather midi
skirt with a slit, and platform lace-up boots. "Wow," Leah and
May had said together, hugging her at the airport. "You're the
one I'd want for my nurse," Leah said.

"Nurse-*practitioner*. So tell me about Daddy. And Nick. But
not till we get to the car. Hey, look at you. My two favorite
women. Mom, you look great. I thought you'd look like a truck
hit you."

"Wait till you see your dad," Leah said. "Oh, not that anything *happened* to him. What am I saying?"

"Daddy." May thought if Vera cried even Leah would cry,
and that would be the end of them. But she didn't, she said, "OK,
so you don't look all *that* great," and put her arm around May
and squeezed her to her side as they walked.

Sometimes, of late, May would feel a dire unrest pulsing from
the person ahead of her in line at the grocery store. Sometimes
she wondered how anyone in the aisles carried the simple load
of the hidden family that was going to eat the groceries, or of no
family, no one.

But then a blast of euphoria would hit her, at the sight of certain faces on the street, certain gaits, a dog wagging for its non-
descript master, the way a woman pushing a grocery cart of her
earthly goods stopped to light a cigarette—a sense of the strength

it took to live and the shocking but finally satisfactory ways so many found to do it. This dizzy, momentary approval of everything that met her eyes frightened her because it might be similar to what Nick experienced with drugs, and who wouldn't want that? Who wouldn't seek it out?

It was her age. All of it. She was at that age. Although some of it might be that she was quitting smoking again.

Her older daughter, Laura, who wrote for the newspaper and had this year won a prize for her series of articles about midlife, had given her a spiral notebook and told her to write down whatever came to her on these occasions. Laura knew of May's solemn ambition as a child to be a writer herself. And later, in high school, May's prize. May had won it for her project on Hooverville. For each of several invented residents of that encampment she had imagined a life story. May would be the first to admit that the students in her own English classes wouldn't even try to get away with such a thing. They had tape recorders; they recognized the preeminence of reality. Absurd as it was, the work of a fifteen-year-old locked in daydream, May had never thrown away the sheaf of onionskin with its brass-plated paper fasteners. Laura had found it and taken it into her possession. Laura was the repository of particular facts about each member of the family, the one trusted not to make light of some unlikely honor or some forgotten pledge or aspiration. "Who knows what you might do with it, if you write down these ideas you're having."

"Hardly ideas."

"OK, it will help you," Laura said.

"How do you know that?"

"I don't know," said Laura. "Just try it."

Right away May lost the notebook, and that was the end of that. She hoped it wasn't lying around somewhere in the school building; she didn't want her students finding "ninth grader changing baby in bthrm, patience, happiness, slvr thumb rings," and screaming out, "That's Mrs. Nilsson's handwriting!"

May had not always been a person who went back and forth, readily exchanging one mood for another, or sank under the weight of an apprehension of the future, or looked at a question from all sides. At one time she had been single-minded. She had been a person who acted, who seized what seemed defensibly hers.

"Wasn't I?" she asked Leah. "But you didn't know me when I was young and wild."

"I've known you long enough."

In love, for instance. An experience, May had found to her surprise, so enveloping at times as to exclude even the lover. She had been in this state with Cole, long ago. Alone in the spangled dark of shut eyes, she had counted over the coins of her passion. But there—the man in the bed with her. Ah, back into his arms, words found, tokens given to stand for the inner state of blank, electrified being.

With Cole, at that time, it was almost always night. Night and secret. May could remember opening her eyes and watching for a long time in the dark as his hands, chapped from too much washing in the strong surgical soap, took shape on the blanket like lights slowly coming on. He was a surgery resident and she was twenty years old, a day student at the state university, work-ing in a lab at the medical school.

They would lie in bed listening to news of the war. They were always in bed, as she remembered it. She was still living at home and she could concoct explanations for her father but her step-mother knew why she was away at night. Of course she did.

She liked the way his hands lay half closed; she liked to feel herself moving very slowly in an element heavier than the air of her real surroundings. She felt at once old enough to stand up to anyone who tried to advise her, and ignorant of the simplest thing, ignorant of how to do all the things she was going to be expected to do. She would look out of her suspended, revolving self at his hands, as if she were looking out of a casement window. Then she would close the window and be in the shuttered room of happiness.

They were not married and did not know they would be. She was eight years younger than he, an eternity to both of them. There was a woman expecting to marry him, someone May had to deprive and punish. She had no reason to honor the woman's claim on him; she knew her only by sight, in the corridors of the hospital.

Cole did not seem to her to have a role to play in this contest, even though he had started the whole thing by letting her kiss him on the cheek, just grazing the mouth, the day the nurses brought in a birthday cake for him. And by following her after that, down to Receiving in the basement where she picked up lab supplies, and kissing her again and maneuvering her into an alley behind packing crates on dollies, against a wall, and pulling up her sweater and going into a ravenous hunt all over her. The quiet, the severe—whether shy or arrogant—Cole Nilsson. The blue-eyed, piano-playing, much-chased Cole Nilsson, who was spoken for. Engaged. And then gasping with her less than a week later in bed.

May was surprised at her determination, unyielding as a

child's: he had to come to her. Marriage, having children—she didn't think of any of that. He had to come to her.

There was a black telephone on his bedside table. How many times his hand went out to clamp it during the night, when the hospital called. The telephone was part of the scene of their bed, with the little clock reflected in its black side. One night when the phone rang it was his fiancée, asking if she could come over. She was a resident too, just finishing up in the ER after midnight. "It's so late," Cole told her. "I have to operate in the morning." He dropped his hand across his eyes and when he replaced the receiver he did it softly. "She's a good person," he said distinctly, into the dark. "You're practically a child. I've got to—I've got to . . ."

May agreed. He needed time. And she argued that if she was able to understand this need, then surely his fiancée, with her hair hanging coiled in one of those woven nets, and her lipstick, and her lab coat pulled tight over her low-slung rear because she walked with her hands in her pockets, so what if she was smart, the only female resident, lots of people were smart—these opinions May did not include—surely she would have to understand it. The good person he was always describing would be patient with the trouble he was having.

They went on in the dark, in this ancient conversation.

He did not need to see her face to know the falseness of what she was saying, or that it didn't matter to either of them who was good and who wasn't. They thought only, at this stage, of each other's bodies. Or not even of each other's, but of theirs together. They were dimly aware of a force shoving out from each of them, clearing things in its way.

In those days they screamed at each other. Or at least May

screamed at Cole. She had reason: for months the woman he was supposed to marry could not be told, because of his anguished, irrational loyalty, and when she was told, she would not relinquish him. Finally she had to, but not before she made her own scenes. Even May felt sorry for her as she went about bringing the locomotive of her approaching wedding to a stop.

What would the patients have said, May sometimes wondered, people with heart trouble who sat respectfully on the examining table while Cole blew on his stethoscope to warm it, if they could have seen and heard these two women, the sobs, the sidewalk ultimatums, and behind them the chorus of medical students and nurses and orderlies who never appeared to take notice of them but knew their story each step of the way?

But the cancellation of his marriage was not the solution it had promised to be. Cole was free, but May had already embarked on a joyless period of seeing several medical students and a history professor from her anarchist study group. The country was not at war but the war colored everything; irresponsible private lives, most of them, were beginning to draw down and hide themselves. Plans had to be serious. Cole was standing ready to join the Medical Corps if war was declared. May opposed entering the war. She was the secretary of her study group; each Tuesday they met at a different apartment off campus where they drank muscatel, read Kropotkin, and discussed the anarchist position on war.

One thing she had learned in the study group was that she was not dependably an anarchist, across the board, and even her pacifism left much for the others to scrutinize. Where was the courage pacifism would require, the pure motive to protect others that she had believed hers by nature? She knew Cole thought her young and selfish, and resolute, and bold: the college student he had followed—who had lured him with a laugh in an elevator, as he recalled it—down onto the Receiving dock. A laugh and a personal remark, which he considered inappropriate.

This made her laugh in later years. "Inappropriate!"

"You have a funny ear" was what she had said in the elevator, out of an unaccountable wish to tease, possibly even humiliate him. She had not even thought it before she said it. Then she clasped her hands behind her, leaned back on the padding—they were in one of the padded freight elevators—and laughed. She was not a person who laughed at anyone else. She would have said she was kind, often entrapped by her sympathies.

This was before she knew his perfectionism, the strictures he placed on himself. Flushed, he had joked, "My defect."

"Well, I'm glad you have one." Would she have crossed the little space of the elevator, touched the folded-down rim at the top of his ear? He claimed she had.

"No, I'd remember that."

"I remember."

Of the study group he said, "You'll go to jail if you're not careful. You don't know who those kids are."

"Some of them are professors. They're people who don't want you killed, that's who they are. And if you didn't even have the nerve to tell *her* the truth all that time, how do you think you could *fight*?"

"It's the Medical Corps, May."

"And I never see you. I saw you more when you were engaged to her."

"I'm a resident. Don't light that. Don't smoke those, May, for God's sake."

They kept this up: they locked each other out of apartments and hotel rooms; storming away from her he ran his car, his prized '33 Ford with the first dashboard radio, off a ramp sideways and bent the axle; they threw dishes, or May did, against the iron radiators of his apartment. They did a lot of drinking, as others were doing all around them, despite or because of the fact that the country was heading for war. Cole's perfect record as a resident received some black marks.

Then they got married and Cole went off to war. May got a job interviewing conscientious objectors for the Civilian Public Service, men sent to plant trees on the coast and fight fires. At times the war was not even in the headlines. The luck of war passed back and forth inexplicably between the sides. The bomb fell on Hiroshima. Cole came back and finished his residency and after that they had Laura. These events seemed to take no time at all.

They put that earlier period into civilized words; they said in later years how lucky they were to have stayed together after starting off in that headlong way.

Out the window the mountains drew closer. They wore patches of stubble but the slopes did not seem to be logged as heavily as the ones lining the valley on their own side of the border. That side fell away. May felt as if she had put down heavy grocery bags.

"I love this so. Being gone."

"We're right here," Cole said.

"So we are." They drove under the shadow cast on the little one-street town by dark green mountains.

The hotel had three or four wings in different architectural styles, none of them finished, or if finished already falling into disrepair, as if the designers had set out several times with high hopes and then lost interest. Yet the sprawling buildings, connected to the small, vaguely Georgian center like full-grown young still suckling, were not precisely a failure. They were defiantly persisting, not all wrong. The lake in front was confidently beautiful, a calendar lake, disappearing in mist at the far side. Above the mist stood voluminous clouds, like buildings. All this was replayed in the water, a still, blue-green oil.

In the lobby a fire had been lit in the stone fireplace, and girls in aprons were laying white cloths on a long trestle table. Waiting while a line of Japanese couples slowly checked in, Cole watched the laughing, gossiping young men at the desk with a concentration familiar to May. One of them wore a rubber guard on his forefinger and was flipping through the same stack of papers on the counter over and over again. The other had the pair ahead of Cole almost registered, but his hand kept hovering above the stapler as he talked. They had a newspaper on the counter and they were talking about something in it. Somebody had disappeared. "Zip, zilch, nada," said the one with the stapler.

May moved out of the line and away. But the two were nice young men, she saw them glance at Cole's reddened face and get busy.

She stood at the fireplace warming her hands. She was surprised after a minute to see that it was a gas fire; a little pipe at the side of the logs was feeding gas into the flame.

The smoke that had blackened the stones all the way to the mantel was from another era, not from the fake logs crumbling apart so realistically. May put her finger in the spring water running into a curved black bowl set into the side of the fireplace. She could feel the heat in the stones. Her legs tingled. Somewhere deep under the hotel was a hot river insisting its way to the springs for which the place was famous.

Cole, still flushed, was coming away from the desk with both suitcases. She knew she had packed too much and she tried to take her suitcase from him, but he held on. When the elevator came it was a tiny, paneled box. She stopped the sliding grille so he could go in sideways with the bags. "Oh, wait, I'm going to get another key. I mean don't wait, I'll be up in a minute."

At the counter the two young men were bending over a newspaper, absorbed. One of them said to the other, "So, they found the husband. The Russian girl's husband. Weren't you here then? No? I'll tell you. May I help you?"

"I just need a second key. But I don't know what room it is. Nilsson."

He gave her the key and she thanked him. When she went on standing there he looked up and she smiled helplessly. "Oh, excuse me. I just—I'm eavesdropping." He smiled back. He turned the paper on the counter for her and pointed.

> A body found Saturday by hikers in the Sharp Creek area is believed to be that of a Russian teaching in the U.S., who disappeared two years ago, sparking an intensive 40-day search of the area. Nikolai Sobol, of Seattle, Washington, was visiting the resort with his wife, who had arrived in the U.S. two days before, when he apparently wandered off a little-used trail while hiking alone and fell to his death near Sharp Falls.

Officials say numerous guests of the resort, as well as his wife, who spoke no English, aided in the search. Although not a person of interest to the authorities, she remained in Canada throughout the investigation.

Authorities are in touch with relatives in the Soviet Union.

"How sad. Is there a picture? On another page?" There was no picture.

"She stayed here a month, this girl. I was here," the young man said to May, tapping his chest. "Summer job," he added, with a look to say he had not always been here.

"What was her name?"

"Let's see." He looked at the newspaper. "'Nikolai Sobol.' Wait a minute. OK, I'm thinking Olga. Olga. They kept paging her. 'Olga Sobol.'"

She thanked him and went to wait for the elevator. There was no one else waiting. The little car was musty and swung perceptibly on its cable.

In this old, thin-walled part of the hotel, above the water singing and moaning in the pipes you could hear voices. In the room next to theirs a deep voice made a bass hum in the wall, with a woman's voice sounding intermittently as a lighter humming, full of pauses. Insinuation and mood but no words: a kind of hieroglyphics of speech. The hum filled the walls. Lovers away for the weekend. May knew that sound, she had murmured and cried out in hotel rooms.

Husbands and wives. Teenagers yelling in the hall, escaping their parents to go find the pools.

She wouldn't think about Nick. He was with her sister Carrie, he was safe. No one with something to sell him would be able to find him. Carrie would not let someone from his past, the recent past, get anywhere near him; she had promised to go with him if he went anywhere, she would not let harm come to him.

They each sat down on the mattress, testing the old-fashioned coil springs. "Not great," Cole said. As if the bed mattered. For he had hidden his long convalescence away from all the people who said he had come through, all but her, and how was she to approach him, now, with nothing seductive left of her? Under the lily pads of her kindness to him since his heart attack, an old, stirring bog: the past in which they had striven against each other with shouts and accusations, and besought each other in tears, and grinned into the same bathroom mirror, and planned and promised and loved. Those two were their rivals now. They would not go away; they made everything an echo of themselves. And how blindly she had counted on her own appeal, as the heat had risen and fallen between them.

"Look! It says you can order a bed board!" May held up the hotel brochure.

He lay back on the bed and closed his eyes. "I'll be fine," he said. He didn't like any reference to his bad back, let alone his heart.

She read the brochure for a while, looking at the historical map with its drawings of fish, canoes, and explorers falling into the lake in their coonskin hats. The men in the water were laughing and floating, under wavy lines indicating steam. "Want to have tea? It says they're serving tea."

Downstairs, they received their cups of tea at the beautifully laid table. Effort had been put into this lobby in the old building, with its carpets of gray-turquoise and draperies of that beigey rose, almost mauve, just starting to appear in hotels. In the heavy woven upholstery an undertow of pride, a sign new customers had been imagined, people not satisfied with the greens and sun-oranges seen everywhere, people who would require new colors to stand for prosperity and ease.

A harpist was playing on a little harp of dark glowing wood. "Why do they all play 'Jesu Joy of Man's Desiring'?" Cole said as they drank their tea.

"Why not just listen. Or look at the lake."

"Or at the honeymooners," he put in, with a tired smirk, and for a while she did look, with a gradual softening of her mood, at a young couple who had claimed the corner sitting area. They sat by the fire in two fat purple chairs pulled close together, paying everything a fixed attention that fed back to each other without their touching or even looking at each other at any given moment. Not a sleek, traveled couple, she with her ponytail and he in his white socks. An innocent pair, by the look of them, very young, coming away from whatever they did in their Canadian town, the makeshift things May had done at their age, nineteen, twenty. They had to work; they would have lost, even if only recently, the real virginity of never having had a job, they were part of the world, married, looking surreptitiously at their rings. Oh, you'll see, May felt her unmanageable smile signal them. She surprised herself with the vehemence of what she would say if they were to show any welcome to her frank stare, and be drawn slowly over to her, and ask, as kids being stared at by older people never think to, "What is the message you have for us?"

Don't let fights worry you. Don't let shouts and tears and running out of the house worry you, or cruel silence, or astounding breaches and omissions. Was that what she would say? *Don't think in broad categories such as "unbearable." Think of a fish, a salmon, ploughing upstream.* So the midwife had counseled her daughter Laura. *No, up, up—up a fish ladder.*

This is marriage we're talking about, after all. Don't be ashamed of the things you're going to do. It will turn out not to have been all that bad. It will turn out to have been a kind of happiness.

And birth, of course, she would say. Don't forget that. The infants. The pure aural pleasure, as lips with the nursing blister still on them form the *m*'s of what they think is your name, the word that becomes your name. And then they are driving away, the name drives away, it was not yours at all.

Don't let the unforgivable worry you.

The harpist spread her voile skirt, which May acknowledged might have looked better floor-length, so her round calves and little feet in pale stockings and tight pumps, planted on the floor, wouldn't show. But the full-skirted, flowered dress was all right, after all; it went with her white, tapered fingers and her small, emotional mouth.

"Ah. From Bach to 'Puff the Magic Dragon.'" About music, about songs in particular, Cole had delicate, developed feelings. Surgeons were like that. They played the piano. Cole listened to Bach and Mozart, but he couldn't play them; when he sat down to play Gershwin and Hoagy Carmichael and Cole Porter—for whom he said his mother had named him, but May knew his mother didn't know music, and Cole Porter hadn't even become famous then—he played by ear. No one had provided him with lessons because his family had been poor, so he had taught himself. Music, like math, was easy for some people. *Yet you,* May thought, *hear the harp, not the music.* And then, ashamed of herself, she puzzled over which was the right thing to hear.

"Honey," she said, "don't be so discriminating. Try to just—"

"Just what?" But he rubbed his face, he let her take his hand as they gazed across the room at the honeymooners.

They found the husband.

The husband of Olga. *Olga Sobol.* May heard the name repeating itself, taking root in her mind as certain foreign words, usually the names of her students, could do if she wasn't careful. Lately, if the news was on while she was grading papers in the evening, Cambodian names were having that effect. *Lon Nol. Neak Luong.* She heard them in the morning when she opened her eyes—*Angkor Wat, Yeng Sary*—as if they had kept on while she slept.

Perhaps the young Russian couple had come to celebrate. He, the paper said, was already teaching in the U.S. She had stayed behind, perhaps waiting for a visa. A long, thwarted time apart. Something bureaucratic.

Crossing a border would have made her uneasy, on her way to this old hotel. Because she was young she would not notice the architectural mess; each thing that appeared or came to pass would be itself alone, unprecedented.

Imagine setting out from home, a Russian woman, or girl, as the desk clerk had called her, to see your husband, and going home without him. But things like that must happen all the time. People died on vacation. Vanished from national parks, trekked into nowhere. Died in transit, on ferries and trains and in the air, passports in hand.

Olga. In her first youth.

Not beautiful. Dark brown hair, pulled back, a white parting. Glasses. A heavy, drooping mouth that broke open, for her husband only, in a lavish smile. She would be thinking only of getting into their room. Their room in the old part of the hotel, just remodeled and painted a grave, hushed blue-green with some black in it, like the surface of the lake they would see from their window. They would see the color May and Cole saw; it dyed everything. Olga and her husband. Not long married.

The room had a transom above the door. With the long rod he would twirl theirs wide, as if to break the seal of the room. She would find cups in the bathroom and pour some of the vodka she had in her suitcase, and after they drank take her glasses off and then his, put her hands on his chest and kiss him.

A wave of desperation for a child had been rising in her.

Something had happened to him in her absence; he was not as he had been. Something in that city, that terrible country, had cramped his generosity, shut down his passionate talk, his impulsive laughter. His hand was cold and lay loosely in hers; his heat was gone.

He had not touched her in the two days she had been there. Walking, he didn't lean on her when she leaned on him. She had lost her balance, the first time. He kept saying he had to talk to her. But all the way there he had the car radio turned up and told her more about rock music than she could possibly sort out.

The clouds were massed on a darkening sky. The lake, if it moved, had a slow, invisible movement. He was at the window, and she saw his black hair where it grew stubbornly down under his collar. She willed him to turn around and send her the look she knew, out of eyes still as thickly, childishly lashed as the dark eyes of ponies at home, the ones she had led around the park with children on their backs, when she had no other job. Children.

First, bed. Afterward, lying on his back with his hand somewhere on her and his eyes closed, he would be able to talk. She understood that. He seemed to have forgotten that they knew everything about each other, and to have reverted, possibly so as not to shock her by resuming their old ways too quickly, to the formality of their earliest acquaintance. Strangest of all, he had forgotten that she was taller than he. He admitted that. He kept glancing at her and shaking his head, as if she had grown.

She found herself sitting on the bed with her long legs curled under her. She was conscious of her dress, which needed ironing. "Where are the jeans I sent you?" he had asked her. She couldn't say, "I sold them." She wasn't sure what he would do. Because they had been apart so long. Of course the resolution, the awaited plunge into blind warmth, the consent between them to obliterate the year—all of that was awkward, and more so because already postponed. She said his name, but he didn't hear her, he was rattling the window, which was painted shut. Certainly they would have to talk about the problem, whatever it was. He would explain in his harried, confused way and she would listen and try to soothe him. But first, before anything else, the big Canadian bed.

Olga would see the bed in this hotel as large, luxurious, would she not? Or was May thinking of characters in Gorky, or Tolstoy, who slept on stoves and shelves, and on piles of wool, or in threes and fours, in the villages? Of course everything had changed in Russia, and changed again, since Gorky fell asleep in his grandmother's bed. But where was Olga from? Perhaps she was from a peasant village where such things still went on, and her hus-

band Nikolai, the teacher, half-American now after a year—
perhaps he was conscious of something left in her of those days,
something he had not noticed until now.

After she kissed him, he put his glasses back on.

After dinner May and Cole were going to the mineral pools, but
coming into the lobby and seeing the big purple armchairs empty,
they went to sit by the fire.

They had eaten so much at dinner that May thought if they
put on their new bathing suits she would not be able to hold her
stomach in, in the black suit so bitterly and comically searched
for with Leah, over days of store mirrors. While she and Cole ate,
a four-man band had played "Smoke Gets in Your Eyes" and
"Harbor Lights" and "Red Sails in the Sunset," and impeccable
old men with handkerchief points had danced with wives in
cocktail dresses and jewelry, while young couples still in the jeans
of their hikes had waltzed without self-consciousness. She and
Cole had not danced; they had been planning to but when their
coffee was finished he had gone to the men's room and come back
ready to leave.

May watched the implacable gas fire, whose flames did not
dart up the chimney or flake off sideways, or suddenly, craftily
gutter and hiss under the logs, even though they were real flames.
Sometimes a heaviness lodged itself in her chest and back, as if
she and not Cole had had the heart attack and gone through all
the assaults of fists and electric pads and hypodermics and was
now laid out only half awaiting reprieve, as Cole had been.
Almost content to die, he had said, he had dared to say to her,
when he was going over the little of it he could reconstruct.

Almost content to die. And now he kidded around as the scrub nurse snapped his gloves on for him in the OR, as he went running in his new sweats, and gathered the medical students around him, and played the piano, and denied he had suffered, out of nowhere, a stupendous crushing-out of his breath, denied he had suffered anything at all, let alone been *dead*.

For a minute a fury poured through her and she couldn't look at his tired face or any part of him, the leg crossed over his knee or the black socks or the hand on the chair arm. He wouldn't sit long before a fire. And he stood and said, "I'm going up to change. I have a journal article I have to read, it's short, and then we'll go. Or you can go get started and I'll come."

"You go up. I'm going to wander around."

She walked to the new wing, where the carpet was deep and the rooms had no transoms. Here the elevators were big and silent, and the guests came and went with muffled steps, to and from the pools in heavy white robes provided by the hotel. Finally she went out through the lobby doors and stood in the blue dark. Then she followed the sidewalk some distance to the spring, which surprised her with its smallness, a dark little pool bubbling in a wrought-iron enclosure. She took hold of the palings and stood there for a while listening to the sound before she let go. For eons it had gurgled in this way, unheard, when there was no one like herself to foolishly admire it, foolishly seek its endlessly reiterated message.

When she got back to the room Cole had already gone. She changed into the black suit, caught sight of her bare self in the mirror, and rubbed handfuls of the hotel body lotion into her legs and arms. Then she remembered the instructions not to enter the baths wearing any cream or oil, and had to get out of the suit and into the shower. In all her care with packing she had forgotten her robe. There were no robes offered to the guests in these older rooms. He had booked this room for her. She put her clothes back on over the suit.

In the middle of the night Nikolai got out of bed. Olga was mumbling in her sleep, his name and a few garbled words in the intimate Russian he was not used to. She had thrown back the covers and swept the pillows onto the floor, and her long white leg hung off the bed. Tears had streaked her face with the new black makeup she used on her eyes.

In the long corridor the illuminated exit signs winked one by one across the badly fitting pastel sweatshirt she had foolishly carried thousands of miles to him, not understanding that he had been living in a country where such things can be found in grocery stores. He hurried, looking straight before him. He was not wearing a coat.

Olga had heard a terrible thing, if she had understood it.

"We don't know where your husband is."

She stood waiting for the next person who was coming to talk to her. They were looking for someone in the hotel who knew Russian. Possibly one of the Swiss—though why should that be so? She did not wring her hands. She couldn't summon, here in this hotel, on this continent, the gestures from her own country that expressed hopelessness.

They had been looking for him all afternoon. Ever since she convinced them he had not gone for a hike as they insisted, had not left in the morning but much earlier, some time between two, when she slept, and four, when she woke. And that he had gone out under heavy clouds, with the moon hidden, no moon, really, to light him. He had left his coat. He was not a hiker. No, he did not know the terrain.

He had left his glasses.

A couple from Vancouver planned to take her with them in the morning. The plan was for the wife to drive Olga; the husband would drive Olga's husband's car to Vancouver. He thought he knew someone who would then drive it, and Olga, down to Seattle. If she would go. There was some question. Then what? They weren't responsible after that. They were hoping her passport was in order for the border crossing.

She couldn't understand what they were saying but she could get the shape of it. She had her own plan. Trails led up into the mountains but she didn't think he would take a trail. He would be sheltering somewhere on the long, rocky beach bordering the lake, trying to think. In her mind she said, *Don't think*. Earlier, in the night, he had been crying, something he had never done, never, saying things she thought at first he had made up, in the confusion that had come over him in the United States. He tried to make her listen while he described a house he had occupied with a girl, his student, a young girl, a whole impossible existence in this one year without Olga, causing the university to let him go.

Now the lake itself, the water, came into her mind. Spring fed, he had said, like the pools. Why had she not asked how he came to know about the place? Had he been here? She had not known to ask. He had taken her to see the black pool a quarter mile from the hotel, enclosed in a little metal pagoda, fenced away from visitors, who might have jumped in. At one hundred forty degrees Fahrenheit, it sent a slow steam through the bars of the enclosure. You could dabble your hands in the spring water, in a little stone basin with a stainless steel spout, a graceful crook rising out of it, that never stopped running. You could plunge your hands into the dark little basin but you couldn't leave them there: a woman with knobbed and deviated fingers told Olga this, with gestures. Olga did not put her hands in, but now she would never see hands in a sink without thinking of this basin.

That you could love until organs inside you twisted like those crooked fingers, that you could do this and yet not go out unerringly and find him — this bewildered her.

They were showing her a map. A Japanese man was trying to speak Russian to her. See, mountains all around them, lake before them, a lake like a vast, stunted river, sixty-four kilometers in length. Room in it for two islands, room for the sunken possessions of departed Indians, she could see from the pictures on the map's border. Room for those who might take a boat out, one of the boats from the little basin in front of the hotel, without knowing about the lake winds, drawn on one area of the map in brisk, terrifying lines.

She had not gone with the couple from Vancouver; she had stayed on past the three days the Royal Canadian Mounted Police had suggested, causing those in the office behind the desk to inquire about her funds. Everyone in the hotel knew her now, and cleared a space for her around the front desk when she got off the elevator.

When the organized search resumed after lunch someone

reported that she had gone off by herself. She had been seen on a grade too steep for an inexperienced climber. A group of young men from the Japanese bus tour, who had been on the beach with binoculars all afternoon, had seen her on the mountain twice, once on the trail already searched by rangers the first day, and once far above it.

The young men were going out themselves to bring her back. For them, that would be the end of it. But she had almost a month ahead of her, to go out and back and never find him.

May found her way down the yellow-lit corridors into a causeway chilled by open windows, to the echoing rotunda that housed the pools. The lights were very low, coming from under the water of the two pools and lighting from below the dozens of faces and the steam playing on the surface of the water. In the dark she saw a ceiling painted with stars. There was a din of talk in the room, amplified by the water. Foreign languages. It was foreigners, people from older countries, who saw the need of these pools. Even in the dim light she felt the presence of mottled, heavy flesh, limbs that had to be hauled up the wet steps with the aid of rails. She did not see Cole.

Her attention was caught by a couple in the larger pool, which was the size of a swimming pool and brimmed with floating people. It was the boy and girl they had seen in the lobby, the honeymoon couple. They stayed at the edge, with their arms on each other's shoulders. The girl pulled herself up and sat dripping, wringing out her ponytail and extending her leg for the man, the boy, to take. She kept pushing him with her foot. They were completely different without their clothes, at ease and confident. May had to marvel at the girl's skin; it had the sheen of rubber, but with an unarguable, almost sedative beauty added, in the dimness, by the luminous heat it gave off. As the boy pressed his muscular arms along the sides of her leg she gave a low laugh. When he came out of the water to sit beside her he displayed abbreviated black trunks, pouched shamelessly. Across his belly and around his side ran a long, meandering, puckered scar, still red, as if he had been sawn halfway through and pressed roughly back together. The girl leaned on him, locked her eyes on his, and ran her finger along the scar.

He dropped back into the water and the girl slid down his body, having given up the laughs and little pushes. May refused to imagine what had happened to the boy's torso. The way they drove cars—with his learner's permit, Nick already drove that way, fast, unsmiling. They couldn't use the car to influence him because he didn't care whether he drove or not. From here she could see that all of his promises didn't matter, either. The problem was life. He, their son, was not bound closely to it. When they got home they must explain to him, much more clearly than they had, the *obligation* of life.

She felt herself watching the couple in the water with the fixed smile with which people who are not dancing watch dancers. The steam, and the fact that she was wearing her sweater in the heat, made it difficult to breathe. All around her in the dark she heard German and a language she thought must be Dutch. Steam, blasts of cold air when children ran in from the dark courtyard where there was an outdoor pool, loud questions and answers between pools, with a harsh rebound or echo caused by the vast room.

A big woman got into the water with a sturdy, jowly baby in

her arms. She dragged it in slow loops through the water as though she were writing with it. She spoke the German-sounding language, which was not quite German, to a woman with dew-lapped arms who seemed to be her mother. The baby appeared to be asleep. But then she tossed it into the air and caught it under the arms. She and her mother laughed with that European assurance, that unfastidiousness. The baby neither laughed nor cried. Fat as it was, it looked ethereal. Its fists were loose, its eyes were drowsy, its attention turned inward in a state May recognized as having belonged to babies of her own. She had a sudden conviction, gathering everything under its reproach, that she too should be able to take a baby into the water. Why was this not possible? Why was that time gone, unfindable with a baby belonging to anyone else? Why know it only now? The woman pulled the lagging baby through the water again, and brought it up dripping against her ribs and cradled it. *All right, all right,* May thought. She remembered feeling in the afternoon that she must make the honeymooners understand something. But it was not right to try to make anyone understand it, after all.

Where was Cole? She felt her heart begin to pound. She was about to run back to the lobby when she saw him. Suddenly, toward the middle of the circular pool, she saw his back.

It was Cole. There was a florid darkness to the back of his neck, with the blond hair plastered helplessly on it. By the time she got there he had gone in deeper, up to his chest, and she knelt down at the edge and called him softly, but he had settled himself on the third step down, with people crowded shoulder to shoulder behind him, and he did not hear her above the echoes.

She reached her arm through and tried to tap him on the back. A pale man saw who she wanted and spoke to Cole, and he turned with a dazed, unseeing expression in his eyes, looking all around him like a man being awakened from sleep and finding himself in the water. When he saw her his face took on firmness, pleasure.

She had forgotten this look of his, and that was her own doing, misplacing it along with so much else in the merciless forgetfulness, the oblivion of marriage, for he always showed this pleasure when he had been waiting for her and she appeared, did he not?

He called, "Are you coming in?"

"Come with me," she mouthed, almost falling against the damp, broad, water-beaded backs in front of her. "Come. Come back to the room."

"What? Now?"

Men and women looked up at her—they were elderly Europeans, nothing surprised them—stirring the water with their hands, on their faces the benign foreign expression that said everything had its solution, yes, everything, once the first youth was past.

"Come, will you please?"

"Is something wrong?" He was doing as she asked, getting to his feet, water sliding off his shoulders, forming runnels on the loose skin where the arm branched off the chest.

She took his hot hands and pulled him. He splashed her, getting out. "I'll get dressed," he said, almost humbly. "I thought you were coming in."

"No, come with me," she said, staggering up, breathless at having found him alive.

Happiness: Nick

May was first; she put her head out into wet grass and drew a breath of ecstasy. Spring. Her hair clung to the spears of grass and stuck on her cheeks. She was crawling out of the car window, into fine rain and the smell of wet earth.

Nick had moved; he had already said he wasn't hurt. It was just going to be getting out and resuming life, which was flaunting, on this green wet spring day, its power to go on without them. If it had wished, it could have ejected them. They were in a ditch at the foot of a big timber company sign. Above them the company had left a line of trees standing so as to screen a meadow of stumps from the road, and as May got to her feet the trees started up a flickering of all their pale green leaves. It was because they were aspens, it was the aspen's calm applause.

Aspens. Sweet air. Spring.

There was a giant blunderbuss in the ditch with them. May closed her eyes and when she opened them again it was a tree stump, four feet across, spiked with hacked-off roots. Nick was halfway out the car window. "Is it gonna"—twisting himself to see her—"catch on fire?"

"Maybe," she said, hardly concerned. She pushed at the hair stuck on her forehead. Her palms came back slimy and red.

They both hung forward over gouged mud, getting their breath, waiting to see if something more would follow the bashes and thuds still echoing, strange prolonged embarrassment, under the low gray sky.

May caught a movement out of the corner of her eye. From underneath a heap of stumps squeezed an animal, an animal with a bright coat. It shook itself and dropped into a creeping run. At first she thought it was a fox but it was a cat, with its jaws around something large enough to cause it to run a little sideways. It disappeared into the dense firs at the upper border of the meadow.

"See? See the *cat?*" Breath in her somewhere, if she could get at it.

Nick squinted at her, going down on one arm on the steep bank. "You have blood all over your head," he said—tenderly, she thought.

"Not you." That was a relief. It was a relief, the purest happiness, to have her son with her on the grass, safe. "Did you see it?"

"What?"

"The cat."

"Cat? Where?"

"Up there, in the woods. It looked like Keyhole."

"You're kidding, where?" Nick cried, but May found she could not point. The old station wagon lay butted over on its back, not even spinning a tire. She thought, *I'll wait and then lie down on my back. I'll wait just a minute.* Let the rain fall on her face.

She wanted breaths deeper than she could get, but there was a live material in her, an enzyme, and she recognized it: it was happiness.

Ribs, somebody was saying, as she sat shoulder to shoulder with Nick on the ground, and she could feel a jolting in his body as if they were being ratcheted to the top of a roller coaster. She thought if he was crying she should explain, describe her own carefree feeling, but now there were noisy people all over the place. Cars. "I don't know," Nick rasped. The voice wasn't right. She tried to reach past whoever it was to get him by the hand, but they were pulling her away from him, lifting her. She was the one getting the attention. Nick was so alert he had remembered to get the keys out of the ignition; he was jingling her big school keyring on two fingers.

"I don't know." His voice farther away. "What next?"

"You the driver?" another voice, mean, said to him.

Nick didn't answer, but he did say again, "What next, that's what I wanna know."

"Yeah, the kid was at the wheel." Another mean voice. "Passenger seat," and with her eyes closed May could tell the man jerked a thumb at her. "Came off the overpass. Saw 'em go."

A long, busy silence. "Age?" This was said by a woman, who was arranging May's arms along her sides as if to measure a sleeve.

"She's fifty . . . five," Nick's voice said, closer now. *Ha,* May said to herself, complimented. She was older than that. Nick had come in beside her where she was lying; he was picking through her muddy hair, holding her head still with fingers that had the car keys hooked on them. It was inappropriate, as Nick often chose to be, but he was picking something out of the top of her head. It didn't hurt her because her scalp was numb. She felt perfectly happy.

"Just get away, get back," said the first mean voice. "What have you got there?"

"Splinters," Nick said politely. "Just plastic. Not glass." He had obeyed the man and moved away; he never argued. May thought the man might have pushed him.

"Nick, go ahead, get the splinters out." May tried to sit up. "Don't you stop him!" she commanded the head above her, with its mean mouth clamped on a ballpoint pen. Then that head slanted away and a hat brim with a medallion replaced it, and then Nick. How clear his eyes were today, blue in their zinc whites. Not bloodshot. She got hold of his hand with the keys and opened it. "I knew the cat by its tail," she confided. "Isn't it something? Keyhole. Keyhole the cat. All the way out here." For she and Nick were on the Olympic Peninsula, that was it. The next day Cole and Vera were coming. Vera was home for a while; they were going to camp by the ocean, as they had years ago when Nick was a baby.

While they were in the ambulance she told Nick a story.

At the end of the story that had come to her, of Gorky picking the hairpins out of his grandmother's scalp, she felt Nick's attention because the trembling had stopped in his hand that was holding hers. Now that she had him right beside her listening, she would have to think clearly. "My mother read us the whole book. I was little, couldn't read. A grandfather beating a grandmother! But she didn't think it was strange and we didn't either! We didn't think anything was strange. Nick, you can live through anything if you—" If you what? She tried to think. The medic said, "Uh huh. Sir"—that tone everybody took with Nick, because of something . . . something . . . you wouldn't jerk another kid around like that, saying *"Sir"*—"you talk to your mom. Keep her on the channel." *Stay on the channel yourself,* May thought, but she excused the man. She was able to hold two opposing views. When they saw she was going to give them trouble they had let Nick in the ambulance with her. They had a blood-pressure cuff on her but they didn't turn on the siren. There was no traffic. Why had the car gone off the overpass?

Strapped under the blanket you could hear the hum of tires below this chamber all fitted out and performing, as it whizzed along, a series of efficient officey clicks and whirs with a rhythm to them. "Poetry of the machine!" she cried. "That's Kropotkin. Your grandmother was a devotee of Kropotkin." Her teeth were chattering and she was the only one talking but that was all right, she wanted to and the medics seemed to want her to. A pleasant static coursed through her body and limbs. Remarkable to have stumbled on this benevolence. "But on the other hand she wanted to organize the poor. Your grandmother. Of course, when it came to war—"

"Eight five over palp," the medic said to his phone, watching a gauge.

"What's palp?" That was Nick.

"Can't hear it."

"Oh God oh God," said Nick.

"Is he all right?" May plucked at the medic's hand, trying to raise her head to see.

"You stay put. He's all right. They'll cry, don't mean they're hurt."

Nick was crying. But the medic wasn't worried about that, even though he had no way of knowing Nick cried all the time. Routinely. *Unstrung,* as their doctor said, by the attempt every organ in his body was obliged to make, every minute, to combine incompatible chemicals.

"If only his sisters were still in the house," May said to Leah. If only the girls were still there to walk ahead of them, herself and Cole, as emissaries to Nick.

"Nick isn't verbal," Leah had said, very early, for she saw it, the very thing his teachers would say later. But Leah, the math teacher, had expected Nick to shine in math. Years had been spent in search of his learning style, for the something other than language that would reach him. For the extremely nonverbal, something else must be found. And Nick had done that, found something.

As long as he was clean, the thing to do, Vera advised, was worry about nothing but keeping him that way. "Nick is never going to *explain* any of this to us," Vera said. "You might as well give up." It was not as if he were confiding in somebody outside the family. The same silences fell, after all, in the living room when he sat with one or another of his girlfriends. Sly, tangled girls, but smart, they all were; they had chosen Nick. They didn't all go to the same school; they found each other, these particular kids.

More than the boys, the girls, even the worst ones, the ones Vera said would sell anything to get high, had polite talk they could pull out like a charge card. It resembled old-fashioned small talk except that it had a high, reciting note, rather formal and pitched across the room, and it carried a warning—with the grassy perfume crushed from their ponchos, the glaze of sweat on their eyelids, complexions sore with the long agonized kisses May caught sight of—a warning to her to come no closer.

At first, May would recall in the first year or so after drugs arrived in his school in a big way, it was the girls who held on. Unlike the boys, they did not let go of their former selves; they still pressed like kittens around their teachers, giggling, keeping one foot in childhood. For a time they continued, almost apologetically, to do their hair and write their papers and keep their lab notebooks up to date. Nick was the beloved of a whole series of such girls. May and Cole agreed they were merely a new twist on the group Vera had belonged to in high school. No question but that Vera had been lucky in her timing.

Then, quite suddenly, the girls were worse than the boys. They were nothing like Vera anymore. They had swollen faces and they ran away and the police found them in motels. "My sister had you for first period last year," one of them offered blearily every time she saw May. Not English, not a subject at all to them but a time of day, a room, in which May had her hour of infrared, of looking in as you would at slow caged nocturnal hunters unaware of your gaze.

Even for these girls May felt an occasional twinge of liking. They had their virtues. They were loyal. Often one of them would come and sit in the living room with Nick and the girl who had replaced her. Quiet talk between the two girls, urgent, while Nick sat with his head in his hands. May could hear names, names she knew. Some secret trouble. Sacred trouble. An ordeal, something being undergone, described in hushed voices as if the girl they were talking about went running by them, staggering and panting, while they slowly turned their heads to urge her on, the way May would once have stopped what she was doing to send her thoughts to a friend in the hospital in labor. But then a few days later May would hear the name again. "Melissa." "She's gone. They took her down to Arizona." If you had the means, there were private ranches for rehab, by then.

It was Leah who had first uttered the word *rehab* to Cole and May, a word with a casual, harsh sound to it, but later full of a businesslike consolation.

Toward the beginning, even when Nick was known to be stealing and lying and selling amphetamines in school, his teachers liked him—the ones who went back over the schoolday when they got home, and came to conclusions, and took the time to call parents. "I'm sorry to say this, but I knew you and Cole would want to know if Nick missed a test." Later Nick didn't go to school at all any more and this unsought popularity of his did not seem to weigh in his favor with caseworkers and judges.

May took an absurd comfort in the fact that he did not turn savage, like the boy in the paper who painted graffiti all over his mother's house. Nick would never have done anything like that. He never turned on them, or even argued. When she or Cole or both of them had finished threatening him or begging him, he got up with his sorry smile, his promise. He was respectful; he didn't talk back to them.

He forgot them.

That was what puzzled her. *After all, there's only one duty in families, isn't there, really,* she thought in her teacher voice, not a reprimanding voice but a sorrowful one meant to bring a student to his senses, *and it's to remember the others.*

Nick went where they sent him, to one after another of the

quiet practices beginning to show up then, in offices likely to be in the counselor's house. Once he had an arrest record he went to louder, more crowded waiting rooms, where bulletin boards flapped with notices and memos and handwritten index cards— "Need ride to Monroe (reformitory) 4X/mo"—and he disappeared down the hall with heavyset young men in tight uniforms, who were not much older than he was.

"He'll turn it around," her sister Carrie said. "Have faith."

"Have faith? This isn't *pot*. We're talking about things that can kill him, *people* who might kill him. People *he* might kill, kids he supplies so he can get his. Carrie, this is *Nick!*" *Nick. Our son.* Carrie never had any sons; her daughters were grown, married; they had gone through the sixties in their teens but none of the three had stepped off the path of responsible maturing and wandered into the underbrush. "It was different then, even though the kids did all that stuff, they weren't so . . . it wasn't so hopeless. If they had had Watergate, and Allende, they would have found out for themselves, those kids, and yelled about it, don't you remember? They didn't have to just look around and see everybody accept it, they got stoned but they didn't shoot themselves up, did they? The country was—"

"Don't start in on the country. May, honey, listen. You know it's not Watergate. Nick's got all he can do to get his shoes tied right now and get to his community service. Don't make it worse. He worries anyway, about who knows what. Something bothers him enough to make him do this."

But that wasn't true. In their first parent conference the rehab director had said, "Don't look for the entry, in the addict. Look for the exit." With a squeaking marker he had printed the word *exit* on a big pad of paper he kept on an easel beside his desk, and then he flipped the page back with a crackle and went on to the next. He printed several words on that one, and the next, while Cole squirmed in his chair.

But it was useless to argue with Carrie.

"Don't you think it might be worse for him when you go around like Mama did, saying this is unfair and that's unfair?"

"Like she did? Are you kidding? I wish I did. I wish to God I did the work every day that she did."

"Well, you're a teacher. Be satisfied. I know it used to drive me crazy when she went on and on, and now with you it's Nixon, and the war—the war's over, for heaven's sake—and capitalism, and blah blah blah."

"I don't do that at home," May defended herself. "Ask Nick if I do. Ask Cole."

"It's the whole thing. Oh, you can't trap me into arguing with you. And don't try to get into his mind. You have to forget about whatever went wrong." Now she was contradicting herself. May didn't say so. How could Carrie, or anyone, know? But Carrie stopped for a minute and sighed. "There's no one answer. What you have to do is hold tight. They can't get all that far off course when they come out of a normal home life."

"A firm foundation," Carrie's husband Laban added gently. In his position—he was a minister—another man would have been calling attention to the failure of May's family to go to church. But not Laban. May had always liked Laban. At that time he was having trouble with his own congregation, which was made up of young faculty from the university. It might be Laban was behind the times. He conceded that. He had seen good men go stale as preachers. The endless war was over, and Watergate was over, yet something, some normality, Laban said, had failed to run back into the space cleared for it. And the ones bringing their insoluble offenses to his office in the church were the ones who still *came* to church, who had not dropped out. For them too, normality had been mislaid. He couldn't be sure what was coming next.

"Don't get May started," Carrie said.

When he came back from the experiment of living with Laban and Carrie, Nick said, "I asked Uncle Labe how they, uh, pray, at that church. Jeez. I don't get it."

"Did he tell you?"

"He just said, 'I don't know what you mean, *how.*'"

"What about Aunt Carrie? Did she have anything to offer?"

"Nah." He thought it over. "Nah. You know she walks in her sleep?"

"Still? She did when we were little."

"She would pretend like she was getting something to eat. Came right down the stairs all strange, when I was watching TV."

"Mm. Must have been pretty late." May felt a little chill. When they were children her sister's sleepwalking had taken place in the very early morning.

"I said, 'Aunt Carrie?' Didn't wanna scare her. She grabbed that post at the bottom of the stairs and went, 'Oh, Nicky! I just want a sandwich!'" He stretched out his arms and slowly waved them. "Man. The Addams Family."

This was the longest talk May had had with Nick in years.

"And she and Laban look so normal!" They fell to giggling. "Oh, I'm glad you're home. So is your dad. We didn't like this plan at all. It can't be right. We want you here, no matter what happens. Mr. *Penn* says you can leave the city next week to go to

the ocean with us." His probation officer's name was a joke between them.

At least he wasn't crying the jittery, coughing tears they heard
him cry in his room, and he wasn't lying. She had to shut her
mind to the thought that his body, his thin body had been offered
to men for money, men with money for that. Whatever he had
been doing while he was away at Carrie's, he was finding things
to say to May now that weren't lies. It seemed he was trying to say
something that might comfort her. "Aunt Carrie had those night-
gowns like *Little House on the Prairie,*" he offered.

The day he drove away with Carrie and Laban, May had
groaned to Cole, "How did this happen? Why does he have to go
over there? Why do we have to do this?" But Cole couldn't
speak, as Laban's car turned the corner with Nick looking back
at the house.

They didn't have to, it turned out. Mr. Penn said they could
change their minds; living with relatives was just one of the
methods people were trying. No one knew who had devised it.

It was a new world, in which many new things were proposed.

Lots of kids did every drug in sight and came out of it. Her
own students did that, year in and year out. She herself said to
certain students, the ones you could talk to, "Everything you're
going through now will change. You'll look back on it and see."

See what?

"Let me give you an example," she'd say to her students. "I
can drive past the house I lived in during the Depression. Right
here in town. We had chickens! It's a boardinghouse now, near
the university. My mother died there, in that house, when I was
fourteen. Oh, I was in a bad way, I was laid low. I thought life

would never be right again. You'll be the same way: someday you'll say, That's where I lived when I was so messed up. Your children will say, *You?*"

She could see them think about children, about a future. If she was talking to more than one at a time they laughed and pointed at each other and said, "You?" The one or two in the most trouble would not be pointed at, in the subtle etiquette they all obeyed, but they would laugh the loudest, at their imagined selves who would have had to leave so much behind to get to those children.

Nick was eight years old when the cat wandered in. He called Laura and she came right over to see it. She was eight and a half months pregnant. They all thought the cat realized that when it jumped onto her lap and rubbed itself against the dome of her belly.

Her husband Will was in school and Laura, though she had left college after a year, had a job writing about women's interests for the *Times*. Sometimes she came over on Saturdays to see Nick and read them something she had written. Always, Laura worried about Nick. Right away she saw how things were; she said they should keep the cat because it made Nick happy.

Vera liked the cat too; she welcomed anything that might alter the boredom of her senior year. May could take cats or leave them, but already she liked this one, with its two natures: half of it sluggish and old, with a cataract and a limp, the other half sniffing all the corners and pouncing sideways like a kitten. It was an orange cat, brown along the spine in just the way an orange rind went brown. It was stiff in the joints and had a crooked tail and an upturned mouth that gave it an expression of poised approval.

Once they had the cat, the house seemed to pulse with minimal, previously invisible events. The cat looked up, they followed its gaze to a shoot of the chimney ivy that had pushed through the brick of the fireplace and drooped a green bud into the living room. By the suddenly pricked, transparent ears they knew the mailman had reached their block. The cat detected some sound in the wires just before the telephone rang, and turned to look. It studied May's rug, an old threadbare rug in the front hall, with a scrolling, imperfectly repeated sentence of shapes on the border. Cole had brought it back for her from a medical meeting in Cairo. This rug the cat sniffed so frequently and at such length, luxuriating, slitting its eyes, lowering its whiskers on one side and then the other to touch it, that May could almost see the ghosts of other cats, or even camels, rise off the worn fibers. She liked to see the cat's orange length on the rug's faded chalices and vines.

It was a shy, well-behaved cat. If it had done anything unpleasant, scratched the rug or peed on it, or peed in drawers or bookcases the way her friends' cats had done, or brought in a dead bird, it would have broken its own benign spell. But it never did any of these things. They took a picture of it and put up signs around the neighborhood, but no one called. The cat was theirs.

May liked its soft, noiseless flop onto the floor where there was a square of sun, in the room where she sat grading papers, and the little jerks of its head as it drifted into unconsciousness. She would bend down and put her hand on its orange pelt, soft and hot, and feel the unexpected skeleton. Why had they never had a cat before?

The cat had chosen Nick. It liked to knead the small of his back and doze there while he lay looking at his Tintin books on the floor. If he began to wheeze it came forward to investigate, and leapt away from the hiss of his inhaler. If he cried, it found him, and climbed up to sniff his tears. It offered no comfort, just the verifying sniffs. May thought, *It must have come from a house where the children have grown up and gone.*

"It's mine," Nick said. Right away he had the cat on his bed and his asthma worsened.

"Why don't we say 'she'?" Vera demanded. "We all say 'it.' It's a girl." Though it had taken weeks for them to find out one way or the other.

"*She's* a girl," Nick said. But the cat remained *it*. A particular sex did not suit it, even Vera agreed.

"Why haven't we ever had a pet?" May asked Cole. He shrugged and said, a little plaintively, she thought, "I don't know, I grew up with dogs *and* cats." It was as if he had confessed an earlier, more complete life. Not having had a dog or a cat in the house while two out of three children grew up seemed to May something inadvertently, almost fatally left out, and magically remedied at the last minute. Thus the cat, with the lightest of blows, broke the past off in a chunk that sailed away from them. Now they were a family with a cat. May thought she read in its little half-smile, *I have come.* Rarely did she let superstitions take hold of her like this, even though she was getting to the age for them.

Laura put the rosy baby up to her shoulder and he burped. "You don't even have to pat him," May said, marveling. "We always patted and patted."

"He just burps," Laura said, not taking credit. She was a calm mother. Most of May's friends thought Laura had landed on her feet after dropping out of college and marrying so young; they thought she had come into the rightful, if slightly tarnished, heritage of girls like her, born for motherhood.

"It's weird," Vera said to Laura. "Don't you sometimes make a mistake, with a baby? Don't you ever . . . not drop it, but put it down wrong? I mean, don't you every once in a while poke it in the eye? I don't think I could ever—"

"It's a *he*," said Nick.

"She practiced on Nick," May soothed Vera.

"Who did? Who practiced on me?" Nick opened his eyes. He was on the floor with the cat on his stomach; he was lying on the sheet he was supposed to be tearing into strips to make a mummy costume for Halloween. He was almost nine. His asthma was not entirely to blame, May thought, for his inability to finish anything. It could be any number of things. It might be this year in particular, 1969, with the war on TV.

From the table where she was working on her lesson plans she would call, "Don't watch that!" to the straw-colored back of Nick's head, on a thin stem like a lollipop. The screen in front of it was a blurred tropical green, with smeared vacant faces of soldiers staring out. She took him with her on peace marches, and Vera's boyfriend Cliff, who was preoccupied with his own draft status, had the idea of starting a CO file for him. He brought them a manila folder and stuck in Nick's drawings of smiling robots. "You keep these guys, man. These are peaceful robots. This is your *future*, man." But—all the mothers of boys said the same thing—the snapping of rifle fire on TV drew out of Nick an answering sound, the way a call is drawn out of a bird by another bird.

More than her daughters, whose bad habits she had worked on in the sturdy rote of the previous decade, this youngest child seemed to May bound by laws that were not necessarily hers or Cole's. Not the plain, everyday, arrived-at laws of the house at all. Maybe the mystery he was to her was simply that he was a boy. Though Leah had said, "Be *glad* he's sort of inactive. You're not twenty-five. This is not a kid you'll ever have to chase down off the high diving board." Or maybe because he was the last, and born after such a long gap, and by some catch and then a compensatory give in events, he was first a stranger to May and then gradually—Leah made a case for it—secretly, deeply favored. "Luckily your girls don't see it," Leah said.

"It's not so much favoring as *carrying*. He won't *steer* the way the girls do. This one's a passenger. I have to carry him."

"Come see the baby?" May coaxed him. But he didn't really acknowledge Laura's baby. *He* had been her baby. If Laura missed a week, he asked when she was coming, but then when she did come he hid in his room.

"You don't have to, Nicky," Laura reassured him. "This little guy will be following his uncle Nick around soon enough. Bring that sheet over and I'll tear too. I hear you picked the cat's name."

Keyhole, Nick had named the cat, for the habit it had of rising delicately on its hind legs at the doors and stretching up as far as it could to sniff at the doorknobs. "It's the keyhole, not the doorknob!" Nick said. "I figured it out! It's trying to see through the keyhole."

"I think we should have named it Felix. Felix the cat," Vera said. All Vera and Cliff read were comics, movie reviews, and books about yoga. Next year Vera would be really gone, there would be only Nick. As a senior she had no work to do and she spent all her time with Cliff, who was already at the university. Cliff was a tall boy with a glossy black braid that reached his belt. Not the smartest of Vera's string of boyfriends. Whenever he was at the house he cornered May in the kitchen and poured out his fear of flunking out and being drafted. But most of the time he lived at the movies with Vera. Vera was going to study film; she was going make movies, she said, that were visually beautiful but political. May had found Cliff rather sweetly and foolishly underfoot until one day she saw him from the upstairs window polishing his Trans Am in their driveway with his shirt off. *Why, Vera's sleeping with Cliff,* she thought. *Of course. It isn't the draft, it isn't yoga, it isn't film. It's the black hair, the white skin.*

"Felix *means* cat," Vera said.

"No, it doesn't," Laura said, laying the baby on his back and holding his clenched feet, letting his head hang off her knees at an angle May would never have allowed a baby. His top lip with the nursing blister on it dropped up to show his sharp little pink gum, and he fell asleep with the ease of a cat. "*Feline* comes from a different root. *Felix* is *happy. Cat* and *happy* don't have the same root."

"So what?" Vera said.

"Is that right? They should, shouldn't they?" May said. "I can't remember my Latin. Surely they're related."

"Anyway, *Felix* is masculine," Laura said.

"I hated Latin." Vera peered at the sleeping baby. "This is just what *you* looked like, Nick. Pale and wormlike."

"I did not!"

"I didn't mean it, this darling child is not wormlike," Vera said, squatting down and putting her arms around her sister's legs with the baby on them. "Maybe I'll get pregnant someday."

"He's not pale, either," Laura said calmly.

The first time they ever turned on the porch light and saw two cops with Nick between them, it was because of the cat.

The cat was not young when it came to them, and the second year it got noticeably older. It slept all day motionless on Nick's bed and in the evenings prowled restlessly with its tail switching, pausing on the hall rug and going on to breathe the dust of each air register, where it would rub against the grille for minutes at a time, drunk on some promise of the heating ducts. It tested the screwed-in metal plates delicately with a claw. "Keyhole wants to go in there," Nick said.

Gradually, though, the cat had stopped coming for its food, and the smelly stuff spooned out by Nick congealed in the dish. "Today it didn't eat again," May told Cole when he came home. "Tomorrow I'm taking it to the vet." But the next day was the day the cat disappeared.

"Cats leave a house for two reasons," Cole said at the dinner table. It was the night after the disappearance. "Convenience or death. As far as I know we didn't inconvenience the cat, so that leaves death. Probably it just went somewhere away from people and houses and crawled into the underbrush. That's what they like to do."

"How do *you* know?" Nick said loudly. He had begun to wheeze. May sent Cole a warning look but Nick was out of his chair. He was ten, getting some growth, and when he hit Cole it was not in fun.

"I know cats. Hey, fella, hold it! Hey, no, it wasn't you. You didn't inconvenience Keyhole. You took great care of him." Cole pulled Nick to him by the fists. "Slow down, buddy. Where's his inhaler? Can't anybody keep track of it? May? It's all right,

Nicky. Slow down. It's a bad feeling, I know. Just breathe—
that's right. Slowly. That's right. We'll all go out tomorrow and
look for the cat. That's right. Slow . . . in . . . slow . . . out."

They were asleep when the doorbell rang. Cole's feet hit the
floor while the ring was hanging in the air.

"I turned on the light and there they were—two cops and
Nick!" They were back in bed. "Jesus!" May held his icy hands.
"I didn't even know he wasn't in the house!" Cole was trembling.
"What is it with him? What is it?" He did not tell her until
morning that Nick had been a mile away in a thickly wooded
part of the arboretum, where the police had found him when
they went in looking for junkies sleeping in the open in the warm
weather.

May had reached the bottom of the stairs in her robe as Cole
was closing the door on the police. Nick was standing on the hall
rug, hands black, face streaked with tears and dirt. "Hi, Nicky,"
Vera said softly from the stairs. The police cruiser started up outside, a red beam and then a blue one probing the stairs. For a
minute all four of them stood there stupidly. May half expected
the cat to come into the hall with its alert, approving look.

"It's three AM," Cole said. He too was speaking softly, not at
all angrily.

"I didn't find Keyhole," Nick said. May took his hand and he
stumbled up the steps. At his door they all hugged him, and they
all went to bed.

Although there were many occasions ahead of them when
Cole would be angry, very angry indeed, that night it was as
though he had been led downstairs in a dream to speak to Nick,
touched on the shoulder by the quiet genie of what is to come. It
was a dulling, anesthetic touch, holding Cole under the hall light

while the carpet unrolled before his sleeping eyes, with all the un-
readable figures in it, of a time when all would be known and en-
acted in full, when even his own fury at what came into the house
with this son and tore them from their beds would be woven in
and smoothed away.

"I've had the most amazing experience," May said. "I've seen the
cat." She said it to Vera and Cole, who had been planning to meet
them at the campsite the next day but had arrived before she even
sat up in bed and saw where the ambulance had taken her.

"OK, Mom," Vera said. They were crowded around her bed
in the little hospital. "OK, if the cat was ten when it left, and
there's no way it was that young, it would be pretty much seventeen now. Right? It couldn't be Keyhole, Mom. And how would
it have gotten over here?"

"Well, with anybody who had it. You see people on the ferry
with cats in the car. Remember how it came to us? Maybe it went
back to its real owner." But of course they knew it hadn't. Laura
had traced the cat.

Seven years ago, for Nick's sake, Laura had walked the
neighborhood for hours with the baby on her back, looking for
the cat, and quite by accident she had found the couple who had
lost it. This became one of their family stories. The cat had run
away from a house not far from theirs, in the same neighborhood
but outside the perimeter of news that might pass on the sidewalk. Laura had struck up a conversation with a woman who
was gardening, who had noticed her a time or two, walking with
the baby asleep in his pack.

"What a peaceful baby," the woman said, getting to her feet

with her trowel. "A boy, isn't it? He must be about, what, fifteen months?"

"I told her I was looking for a cat. Well, neither of us could believe it—it's their cat. She described it exactly. They're the couple in the stucco house where we used to go over the wall when we were little, remember, Vera, because it was empty half the time? That's because they go abroad. They go and live in Malaysia. In Kuala Lumpur. I love that name. They brought the cat back with them from there."

In the garden behind the wall, Laura had had a long talk with the couple. They kept her at the wrought-iron table for hours, talking about Malaysia and their son who was in Vietnam. He had left school for one semester and been caught by the draft. The husband said the son knew full well that would happen if he dropped out of school; the wife disagreed.

Both were certain the cat Laura was describing was theirs. It was the same animal: their cat could hear a crumb fall. "She could smell tears." The wife said that, a big, reserved woman. "And she always tried to get to the keyholes, because the house in K.L. had those deep keyholes for skeleton keys. Remember, Jeff? The little bitty house lizards laid their eggs in them."

"I'd go to Malaysia just to see that, wouldn't you?" Laura had said to Nick when she first told the story, sitting with her arm around him. "Everything she said made me want to go."

On the flagstones in the couple's garden lay a little dog, which Laura made much of. The husband said it was a good thing they had a dog now, a dog would never take off the way a cat would. A dog would be harder than a cat to farm out, though, when they left the next time. He rolled the little dog over on its back with his foot, and kept it there with his shoe on its freckled belly.

"What a prince," said Vera when Laura was telling the story.

Laura said, "It was one of those toy breeds, with the tail fluffed out over the rear end like a wig. It was a *little* dog. Smaller than a cat."

A strange thing had happened in the garden: when the husband let the dog up, several crows at the top of a cedar tree began dive-bombing it and continued for several minutes, screeching and plunging, until it crept under a chair.

"Oh, stop it! Stop it!" the woman had suddenly shouted out, flapping her arms. "I don't know what's gotten into the birds. I swear I think they're poisoned with something. I don't know what's gotten into anything!" And she had doubled over in her chair and begun to heave with sobs, right there on the flagstone with glasses of iced tea and her husband chuckling with embarrassment and patting her on the shoulder. It was because of the son, Laura said, the son in Vietnam.

Laura got up to leave, and when the husband offered his wife no comfort and went back into the house pushing the cart of glasses, she tried to say something about how the war was affecting all of them. The woman had picked up her trowel and she waved it despairingly. "But do keep the old kitty if you find her. Jeff never liked her all that well. Her name is Madu, did I say that? *Madu* means honey. For her color."

"Or," the husband said, coming back out and raising his eyebrows at Laura, "it can mean concubine."

"Oh, we shouldn't keep her," Laura said.

"Please do," the woman said. "Two animals are too many for us."

"Why did it?" Nick said. "Leave their house and come to ours?"

"Probably because they got a dog," Laura said.

"Our house was better," Vera said.

In the hospital room Vera gave up arguing about the cat May had seen in the field of stumps. They didn't want to tire her. The word was not in yet that there was nothing really wrong with her, and none of them knew she would be released the next day as if nothing had happened. They were coming back later to see the doctor; right now they were going out to get something to eat and find a motel.

The next day May was fine. Three of her ribs were broken, but the cuts they had sewn up in her scalp were superficial, and her sensorium, as the doctor told Cole when he knew he was talking to another doctor, had returned to normal. She was lucky she had had her seatbelt on, the doctor said. Mother and son were both lucky. It could have been a very different story. The whole family was lucky.

They felt lucky. They had a couple of days at the ocean but they didn't camp. It rained and they rented two tiny cabins, but crowded into one during the day and played the old board games they found on a shelf. Looking out at the rain they talked about the accident and the little rural hospital and the good luck of seatbelts and helpful bystanders.

May talked about the strange happiness she had experienced as she climbed out the car window. Nick joined in the talk. Or they all said later that he had.

Coming back from the ocean, Cole and Vera always sang in the car, songs Cole had played on the piano for the girls when they were little. Heading for the ferry they sang "Bury Me Not" while Vera acted it out in the back seat. She got herself going on the death-slumber, on the mother's prayer and the sister's tear. She acted "Jeanie with the Light Brown Hair" while Cole sang:

I hear her mel-odies, like joys gone by,
Sighing round my heart o'er the fond hopes that die:
Sighing like the night wind and sobbing like the rain,
Wailing for the lost one that comes not again.

People in other cars glanced over at Vera pulling her hair and wailing in the back seat. After that they sang some more and laughed arbitrarily at whatever anyone said. "Stop!" May said. "It hurts my ribs."

Vera said, "It's too much for her sensorium!"

It seemed to May, thinking back, that Nick had laughed as hard as any of them, but she could not be sure.

On the ferry, people looked at them: May's bandages, the noisiness of Vera. And Nick—where was he? Vera pointed. May went out onto the deck. When she got to him at the railing fear began to turn in her like a slow fan. She knew to look at the hands, the eyes, though he had his hands in his pockets and his collar up in the wind. He had his eyes shut. But he couldn't have used anything before he drove off the overpass. He had been with her the whole time, where would he have gotten it? "Don't worry," she said.

"What about?"

"It wasn't your fault."

"Right," he said. "Right, right. Even though you know I was high."

"No, I didn't know that." She looked down at the volume of water being churned up by the ferry.

"So if I had killed you . . ." he said finally.

"But you didn't, did you?"

"No." He turned and smiled. It was the smile she called his courtroom smile, of bleak politeness. She would remember it sometimes when a student passed her a test paper with none of the blanks filled in. "Don't help me," Nick said. "Don't help me with my alibi."

The night before she left the hospital, the Friday night, as the three of them were saying good night to her, Nick had suddenly spoken. From the chair where he had been slouched all afternoon he had said, "Hey. I saw it too. The cat."

They could have ignored it. At that point they were all exhausted. But Cole went and stood behind the chair where Nick was slouched bruised and stiff, a big vinyl chair you could tip back and sleep in if you were staying the night in a patient's room. Cole said, "Maybe we should go out there in the morning before we come back here, and look for it. What do you think, Vera? They both saw it."

"Why not?"

"Believe him," the caseworker had said, the latest one, with the honeyed voice that none of them could stand. "Give him the gift of your belief."

For a long time May did not really keep up with Nick. She slid farther and farther behind, and not because she couldn't see what was going on but because she was occupied in the same way his teachers and counselors were, with the problem of his future. That was it. One day Vera said in exasperation, on the phone, "He's in a *halfway* house, Mom, for God's sake, he isn't going to *take* the SATs."

By the time May was taking it a day at a time, as the case-worker said to, there was nowhere to turn a beam of optimism, if you had kept one, but onto the body, with its two legs, its two arms, its skin, its bloodshot, sunken blue eyes, its blond hair. The body was alive.

That was not so unreasonable.

Three things made her think Nick could not die. He had accidents but he came out of them unscathed. No matter how down and out he was, in the face of calamity he rose up willing at least to defend himself, not passive the way he could be for months at a time. She had seen him come up out of a basement cell into the courtroom every bit as shaven and combed as his lawyer, and hold himself so still no quiver could be seen to pass over the too-big suit from his sophomore year that May had taken out of the storage bag and ironed. And third, he had told her he wouldn't. He wouldn't die.

If anyone ever asked her the happiest day of her life she would not say her wedding, or any of her three births, or the heights she might reach unexpectedly on a spring afternoon with her favorite class of eleventh graders, her class in autobiography that everybody wanted to take because they thought it was easy, reading the end of *My Childhood* where Gorky has someone say, "We all die, even birds," just before he writes, "And so I went out into the world." Or on a different plane, the night in another city when she paid her first stunned attention to the eyes of the man who was to be her lover, or even a morning sharp with sun before her schooldays ever began, when she went out to feed the chickens with her father, or a day her mother chased her into some cold, flashing water and picked her up dripping and said, "You are my *real* darling."

Of course you would not be able to pick the happiest day in a life, she would say. Though its opposite, you might. Even doing that was unlucky. It supposed the list was already complete.

There were too many different kinds of happiness, too many occasions for it. It sprang up in every soil. In no soil. Like ivy, it worked its way through brick, no matter that it might be a silly, upstart, last-minute thing. There was the unshared kind of happiness that you could feel when you opened a certain letter, though you could make no outward show, and there were long-awaited, ceremonial happinesses, like weddings, requiring sober preparation. There was selfish, hoarded pleasure, offering itself in the wrong place; there was exuberance that flared up hissing like a camp stove. There were risks, mistakes. Mistakes could certainly carry a wild happiness. In a life like hers, a life impossibly protected and fortunate as you looked at lives around the world, a life burst open and pumped out and then stubbornly, appallingly reverting to something that would have to be called happiness— you could never choose one day. But if someone made her choose, she would say, The day Nick and I were on the Olympic Peninsula on our way to the beach, when he was seventeen, and we hit the shoulder coming off the overpass and rolled, the spring day when the aspen leaves were shaking and there was an airy rain, the day we didn't die, the day we saw the cat run up the meadow of stumps into the trees.

The Penitent: Arne

It was almost time for another note from Arne. Arne, the penitent. May said so to her daughter. Was there anything? "No," Laura said. "There's something from Aunt Carrie but nothing much else. Leah called, of course. Why don't I just call Arne, see if he can come by? I think Jackie's coming, from your office, but that would be OK. They'd get along."

My office, May said to herself. She didn't ask to see her sister's note, and try to decipher it or have it read to her. *I never gave my office a thought. I must have been worse than they said.* She had had a small stroke. They said small.

"Oh . . . don't know. Funny . . . no card." In her desk drawer she had a rubber-banded packet of greeting cards, lighthouses and flower gardens and moons, and inside, the rounded, childish signature, two big rings, A and O, for each year Arne Olafsson had lived after chasing her son into the lake.

In the shut drawer, even now, they rave and grieve. That was a poet. Letters in a drawer . . . a woman poet. Since the stroke, May had devised a test of her memory, with lines from songs and poems. She still had a stock of them but in many cases she had lost the source.

When was the stroke? Laura had flown in from Malaysia, then her husband Will, and was it days or weeks since they had first appeared? They were both in May's apartment, and had been. May felt obscurely detached from the whole episode of the stroke, deleted so cleanly from her memory, and she was unmoved by it, as if she had stayed behind in the car while someone else went out to meet it. " 'Stayed in the car with the door shut!' " she heard Laura on the phone, quoting her.

Any day now another "Thinking of You" would come from Arne, with the carefully varied wording that told her he kept drafts of these yearly requests for her blessing. A man of boyish, stupefying sentiment—what cruelty his first wife had shown, to divorce a little boy—whose mother must have borne in on him some Norse lesson about saying you are sorry, so that he could never be finished with it.

It turned out he was a relative, a distant relative of May's, by marriage. "My stepmother was an Olafsson," she had whispered, twenty years ago, in the middle of the night in the police station where they had had their first sight of Arne Olafsson and his dumb tormented blush. Around the state, the Olafsson family numbered in the hundreds. But it turned out there was a connection; an aunt of his brought out the family Bible, he told May, and proved it to him.

Another phone call, to be made by May in response to the note. That familiar jostling audible through the receiver as the man shifted from foot to foot and blushed over whether he could expect it, whether May was really required to come one more time to the café where they met each year. One of his wives had become a friend of hers, but Arne himself made only this once-a-year approach. They met under the freeway, with the roar above them and the whine and vapor of diesel saws drifting in from a little lumberyard next door, in a place where the waitress knew all the cops.

The same big-armed waitress every year: she knew May and Arne as a pair. This waitress knew, May felt she knew, the steam built up in Arne, making him rattle the lid of the creamer as he poured, and fish out the wet sugar packets he dropped in May's coffee. The waitress knew May's flat acceptance of these wild surplus courtesies, and let it be known that she did not admire it, her sympathies were with the male. She poured their refills with her chin tucked, and the knowing, put-upon smile she offered every table.

May liked to get there first and sit in a window booth so she could catch sight of Arne, in the black sunglasses he wore rain or shine, as he eased his bulk out of the car and headed across the street to meet her. He had gotten fat. He had a desk job, now; it was years since he had pulled up in the blue cruiser.

Once in a sunny October when they were getting to know each other he had said, "You want to take a ride?" On the streets she liked the way all the cars slowed down in the vicinity of his cruiser, but Arne had a heavy foot when he got on the freeway and she was glad when he took the off-ramp.

His black boot was a size 13. So heavy it would in all likelihood have embedded itself in mud somewhere just off the pier, once it came off. She knew each inching, stuttering frame. She knew the minutes, the seconds. Once he got one boot off he quit hopping and tearing at the other and dived in, and the stuck one filled with water and came loose. Proof, no matter what anyone else recalled or did not recall, proof this man had been in the water with Nick, so that Nick had known he was being saved.

Indeed, long before his first note to her, Arne Olafsson had been an intimate of May's, figuring in every bolt of thought, visiting in dreams as often as any lover, dream witness with dripping crewcut and awful blush to her howls in the night, before Cole woke her and she came to herself enough to be sorry and stroke the tears these nightmares of hers produced on his stiff cheeks. It was unaccountably worse for Cole, who didn't dream because he didn't sleep. This went on for months, years.

Awake, May didn't know what it was that pulled her back from the groaning fullness, the wretchedness, the night tears to which Cole had mysterious access. Whatever it was, it made her say to herself, *Wait a while, wait, for that. Do what has to be done, you'll have time later for that.*

Rescue attempted, Nick's rap sheet said. May wanted a copy and they gave it to her. They had misspelled Arne Olafsson's name. Officer in pursuit: Olson. Yes, when he saw a kid fiddling with a car trunk he had jumped out of a patrol car to give chase, with flashlight and stick. But it was he who had dived into the lake on a thirty-five-degree night and gone on swimming in the black water until they hauled him out by the balloon of his jacket. It was he, Arne Olafsson, twenty-two years old, who had doubled over and hung his dripping head down and wept—his partner told her that—because he had chased a poor junkie too wasted to swim, a kid with a wallet with thirty dollars in it stolen out of a car, to his death.

Cole had met Arne. Cole had joined them, once, in the café

under the freeway, but with him there the little ritual had foundered. He took up one side of the booth by facing sideways, and rather than slide in opposite him, and beside May, Arne pulled up a chair. Arne spilled coffee, the quiet café resounded with the growls of his stomach, he let off gas, like an animal unloading for flight. With Cole he had to start all over again, pounding the Formica with the flat of his hand. "What—the *hell*—did I care, anyway? Do I give a *shit*—if some dumbass lawyer—jogs the lake at night and loses thirty bucks out of his BMW?"

May had prepared Cole: "I don't think you can imagine remorse like this, going on year after year." She couldn't be sure what Cole's feeling was. Possibly that Arne too should be dead. That might have been what attacked Arne in the gut when he saw Cole for himself and sensed in him the shape of a threat, like a cat arching sideways to enlarge itself. The threat of a furious man, an unappeasable man. That was what Cole was, and it was going to turn back on him too, it was going to squeeze off a quarter of the heart muscle he had left from his first heart attack, it was going to kill him.

While she, May, who thought her life was over this time for good, thought she grieved as a rare initiate, was going to live on.

Laura had come to these meetings too, more than once. The first time, she shook Arne's hand, allowed him to hold on to hers while he completed a long, garbled speech, and sat down next to him. Of course Laura would not turn her back on a sufferer— though that was what she had done, she told Arne. She had done it with Nick. "After I had been married a few years I think I let go of Nick. I did. He was in trouble all the time and I just . . . I was having babies."

Arne didn't say, "Girls get married, they leave their brothers." He nodded, he wiped his sunglasses. Laying them on the table he said, "I heard he set a lot of store by you."

"The worst thing I did," Laura said, with the film of unfallen tears magnifying and lightening her eyes, in which May could see Arne lose himself, gradually swaying in her direction in the booth, "was I got used to him as he was. I thought, 'That's Nick.' I got used to him down to nothing, in the halfway house."

"He had a beautiful sister, I'll say that," Arne said.

May had had to caution Laura. "He's getting a crush on you, honey. The man's a bottomless pit. Go easy."

Vera never came to the café, never met Arne. "It's not a question of forgiving. I don't forgive or not forgive. I don't want to see him. I don't want to know what he looks like or where he lives or anything about him and I don't want you to try to talk to me about him."

"I'm not trying to talk to you about him," Laura said.

"Don't even think about him when I'm around," said Vera. "I'll know."

"That wouldn't be an order, would it?" Vera was working on not ordering people around.

"Just never, never try to sit me down with Arne Olafsson."

If she talked slowly, the words came in sequence. "Oh, the . . . what . . . it was the CPS, during the war, what . . . *was* that?"

Laura and Will lingered at the breakfast table, letting her go on. Laura liked to lead her back quite some way, to the part of her life before their family, before anything serious. May obliged, though she would have agreed with Will that her mind was paddling against one subject after another in the mechanical daze of one of those grabbing arms in a souvenir machine.

"Beats me," Will said with a faraway smile, taking his grapefruit skin to the disposal and peering down out of the high window. "Gulls all over your Dumpsters." He couldn't keep from this daily inspection of May's building, with its cracks and plumbing stains. The day was cloudy, and from the table May could see a smudge, an ash-pink moon, in a clear part of the sky above the nimbus of hidden sun. She did not want Will to notice the moon or comment on it. *Come up, thou red thing. Come up, and be called a moon.* There. That was Lawrence.

"They did . . . survey, land survey. I was married . . . but young," she told her daughter. Sending a silent message, *Will doesn't like old women. Be careful when you're getting to be an old woman.* Laura was not young herself, in a year or two she would be fifty. Already she had a grandchild, as May had at her age.

But at her age I still had a little boy at home, May thought with an ancient, absurd pride. *I had all those years to go.*

"Civilian . . . Service. Was that it? Think of the—the whole wartime—"

"Atmosphere," Will said, getting up and looking at his watch. "Well, the stores are open. I'll go get that wrench." He was repairing something under the bathroom sink for May, she was not sure what. "There was a man in it, I'll bet," he called back, in the relief of getting away from the table. He had found something to tease May about, early in his marriage to Laura, and he relied, not unkindly, on the comedy he found in a mother-in-law with a liking for men.

"CPS . . . Civilian Protective Service?" Laura said, waving him out of the room.

Where did this girl (for in her forties Laura was still a girl) come from, with a nature so serene and pitying? Maybe it was because she had been born on the spring lawn of their childish delight at being married to each other, safe together after a world war. Laura would say calmly, "See that?" pointing at a halftrack on TV, one of the Gulf War earthmovers driven over trenches to drown men in sand. "I think the kid next door drove one of those. Poor guy. He's in the reserves. Remember, Vera, the one who cut our grass when Will was away?"

Whereas Vera was afire with bitter theory and had to get herself to the Middle East, she had to be on the spot, carry in medical supplies on her back and drag reporters with her to expose the border guards, the bribe-takers. In the field, Vera had been known to snatch a syringe out of a clumsy doctor's hand.

Vera did not believe in medical school, whatever Cole said, or in submitting to any ordeal except one you picked for yourself on the spur of the moment. "So I fly out on Thursday," she would say, rushing in when Laura was cooking one of her dinners for all of them. "Can Will steal me masks from the hospital? Do I still have a passport? Is it here?"

"It's at Trevor's," Laura would say. "Remember he called Mom to say he had it, when you moved out."

"No, did he?" Things belonging to Vera lay unclaimed in half a dozen apartments.

The surgeon had a way of genially shouldering aside that vague dark thing, the Possible, that had reared up over May. "You're going to do fine. Wish everybody snapped back like this. Wish Cole could see it."

He was a neurosurgeon brought in by the neurologists to

consult. He raised his hand and gestured away, with one grand, crossing-out motion, the chart, the previous consultations, their fears. "Sit up, it's the pope," Laura said the next time they heard him at the nurses' station. He always looked in, because of Cole. He had been a resident when Cole died.

It was unlikely that May would have any further trouble. Possible but unlikely. Further trouble would be *another one*. Well, yes. A bigger stroke was possible.

"Are you all right?" Laura said when May was back in her own apartment. "What do they think? I still don't know, after all that talk the whole time you were in the ICU, and all the diagrams the guy made us. Will says it's because you have him for a son-in-law. I said, 'No, I bet he thinks you're a *lawyer.*'"

"They all . . . all knew . . . your father. Laura, I know Will . . . has to go," May said, leaping ahead.

"He will, Mom. And we want you to come back with us for a while. You'll like it in Kuala Lumpur."

"No. No." Will was teaching epidemiology in the medical school. He worked hard with his students, he met their families and recommended them for grants, he worried about whether he was overemphasizing technology that would not be available to them, he was probably a good man. The family joke was that Cole had singled Will out in medical school, for Laura. "Well, right at the moment, we're here," Laura said. "You might as well get used to it."

"I don't know about room . . ." The apartments in this retirement complex were expensive and tiny. May could hear the contractor: *How much space do they need at that age?* No one she knew in the building had an extra bedroom.

"We can stay indefinitely," Laura said. They were sleeping on the hideabed in the living room. "Will's on leave, we have plenty of time." For Laura there was always plenty of time, she moved in it at her ease. "So, back to the CPS, whatever it was."

"What was I . . . damn. I'm better in the morning." Each day she seemed slower to herself. "Oh . . . they had a foreman! He came, did . . . interviews. With me. For smoke . . . smoke jumpers. I had such a crush! But that's . . . that's what I went in for, as a girl." She pondered. "So much purer and more intense." *Than what?* she would have written beside a sentence like that, in her teaching days.

"Crushes are underrated," agreed Laura, who had married Will at nineteen, while he was still a medical student. May tried to imagine this placid daughter of hers with a crush on anybody. Yet Laura had written a book. Out of nowhere came a book. And then another one, about Malaysia. Out of the blue!

Cole had said to May at the time, "You shouldn't keep saying that."

"But I don't say it in front of her."

"And it wasn't out of the blue," Cole said, surprising May by having an opinion on the subject. "Don't you remember how she had to have a bedtime story?" May could see herself coming downstairs after the girls were in bed, and Cole just back from the hospital coming up, taking the stairs two at a time, still in his raincoat, to say good night. How would he remember, when May did not?

May remembered movies. Westerns. All those Saturday afternoons when Cole was on call, before Nick was born. The fifties. The three of them in the dark, Laura with her knees up, mesmerized, Vera a whispering, squirming thing, sulking at being kept indoors. Looking up at the huge gnashing horseheads, the golden country, the plot unfolding into rescues so sweet and inevitable.

The first book Laura had written gave May a jolt, coming from someone who, unlike her sister, had little to say on many subjects absorbing people just then, such as the war and the pre-election burglaries. And women. Laura went to her friends' houses for consciousness-raising but she didn't try to get May to go with her, the way Vera did. "I do need to change," Laura agreed with Vera, but she didn't change. The book was an extension of a series of articles she had written for the paper about the downward spiral of a family on welfare. It was a surprise to May that those articles, with all their distracting and somehow ameliorating photographs, could have turned into this unnerving little book. What was to be done? Laura did not know, she merely wrote her book.

The second one, about Malaysia, was not a travelogue or one of those smug books about living abroad; it was about the country, such aspects of it as Laura had studied or come to love. It wasn't political enough for Vera, but it got Laura an interview on the radio, where little mention was made of it. "Well, my mother taught English," Laura said at the end of the first question, an inquiry into the motives she might have had for writing a book at all. The interviewer did these shows on the radio and he wrote reviews for the newspaper. *Why, he's envious,* May thought, listening. In answer to his insistent questions about the first book, on the welfare family, as it related to herself and her background, Laura said calmly, "Are you saying were we on welfare? No, we weren't."

"Playing devil's advocate," said the moderator, "you make a lot of allowances for those who don't work. The one you call Stogie, the father in your first book, is a—"

He waited for Laura to interrupt him but she did not. She let the pause drag on. He had other points to raise and never got to the book on Malaysia, May remembered that, though he read a paragraph of it as the music came up at the end of the show. He read a passage about the house lizards. Laura didn't seem to mind.

"Now I'll clear up, and why don't you take a rest, Mom? People are coming by later, so this is a good time to rest."

May lay back in the armchair. The pink moon was gone, the sun had broken through to make a glare on the wall, with her profile in it, the hair floating up in all directions. She narrowed her eyes drowsily. "You were the one, you liked to make shadow animals," she called clearly, her first long sentence of the day, to Laura in the kitchen.

"What?"

"On the wall. In your room."

"Oh. I thought you were accusing me of . . . I don't know . . . vagueness," Laura said. "Making shadow animals."

Oranges. May could smell them in the air. A scarf of orange scent was being drawn back and forth in front of her.

"Mom, guess who's here?"

They had been talking but it seemed she had gone to sleep. She struggled awake, her hand going to her hair.

"Arne!"

He knelt by the chair. She put her fingers on the "Reno Air" logo on his jacket, and then on the white bristles of his crewcut and the soft tanned skin of his cheek, pocked like a golfball. Through the tan came the blush of his endless shame. "Arne, you came to visit me."

He looked over at Laura, not sure whether to say she had sent for him. "It's that time of year," he said.

In the fall, when the pavements were bright and full of reflections and streams ran in the gutters, May would observe how many objects lay around in the streets. Not just hubcaps but soggy bathmats. Paperbacks caught on grates. Tennis balls, blocks from any court. "Tennis balls just have to be free," Vera said. Nick had the answer: dogs dropped them on the way back from walks. The light would change, the leash would tug, the dog open its mouth, the ball roll into the gutter. Nick had discovered this one day when he happened to be sitting on the curb beside a park for a long time.

Umbrellas. Doorknobs. Oven racks. A telephone book.

One big-soled running shoe, on its side. That was the most common. If she drove across the lake on one of the bridges without thinking of Arne's boot in the water, it was not because she had left off imagining it.

For a long time, years, she had obeyed the impulse, no matter where she might be in the car when it came, to get to the lakefront quickly and drive along the water. She no longer did that. She had had a particular hill for her approach. As you drove down this hill, Mount Rainier loomed beyond the lake in the center of the windshield, an immense pyramid of snow on a platform of air. No connection to earth. The mountain-that-was-God, the Indians had named it. What do *we* have? she had moaned to herself, turning downhill and suddenly seeing it after it had been shrouded in mists for weeks. The *what* that-was-God?

When people asked how many children she had, May said, "Two," or "Two daughters." Gradually the necessity of explaining had abated, just as later, when she was a widow, the compulsion to offer proof of the years she had been married would sink away. That was all right. That was as it must be. Eventually the past went from being cards laid face down to cards not held at all.

Someone was tiptoeing into the room, as if May were asleep, when in fact she was wide awake, talking to Arne. A very tall girl, a beautiful girl. Behind her a spray of feathers. Not feathers but a huge bouquet, full of ferns, nodding in Laura's arms. "Hello, hello," the girl said to left and right, though there was only Arne there with May. He jumped to his feet. The girl had a peculiarly soft, hushed voice.

May stared for a minute, and then, thank God, grasped who it was, it was Jackie from her office. How could she not have recognized Jackie?

Laura set the foil-wrapped vase of ferns and tiger lilies on the coffee table, with a smile that told May she remembered the stories of Jackie. May had sent Laura a chronicle of her experimental year in the office—funny, savvy letters, she thought as she mailed them off, offered as proof that she was on top of things, able to leave retirement behind her and learn computers, able to get along, make friends, amuse and be amused.

In answer to her descriptions of Jackie, Laura had sent her a Malay phrase for *clumsy*. It was long, perhaps it was a verse. May couldn't remember it but it meant something like "Big as the earth may be, I miss it if I try to hit it."

Jackie. She had missed, without knowing it, the sight of Jackie making her way through the office with yellow Post-its fluttering around her, sweeping folders off people's desks with her hip. The gait, all her own, with which Jackie now advanced, awkward yet delicate, like a loaded camel led on a bridle. "May? Honey? It's Jackie."

"Jackie, how wonderful! But I can see you."

"Well, I wasn't sure. I didn't know, I thought I would make sure because—well, at the office? We weren't sure?" Jackie put up her shoulders in her high, countrified shrug.

"I haven't forgotten . . . anybody, in one week."

"Oh, May. Don't be mad but it's a month." When pushed, Jackie would stand up for herself. She sat down, took May's hand in hers, tenderly pressed little pleats into the thin skin over the knuckles. "Oh, and I brought you a book, I don't know, it's just a paperback," she said, putting down May's hand to rummage in her purse. "It's probably no good," she said humbly, to Laura. "I wish I could find a copy of *your* book. The one about, where is it you live? To read, I mean."

"There might be one around here somewhere," Laura said kindly, making no move to find it.

May held the book between her palms before she looked at it. It would be *Love, Medicine and Miracles*. But it wasn't, it was a novel, with a young, long-haired woman not unlike Jackie on the front, her face and body embossed like the title. "Thank you. Have you read it? And tell me . . . about the kids."

"I didn't read it but I heard about it. It may be too . . ."

"Romantic? Spiritual?" May said, her mind suddenly quite clear, even cutting.

"No . . . just . . . The kids—fine, I think. *He* has them this week. I'm Jackie," she said to Arne, who was staring at the silky hair she had gathered into one hand and strewn back over her shoulder.

"Jackie, this is Arne Olafsson," Laura said. "I'm sorry I can't remember your last name."

"Hmm," said Jackie, without supplying it. "Pleased to meet you, Arne."

Laura brought a tray of coffee cups and the cake that had been sending the teasing smell of oranges through May's sleep. "Arne is a cousin of ours," she said to Jackie, passing the plates.

"I . . . think I know," Jackie said, with her finger to her lips like a child who knows the answer to a riddle.

Arne merely ducked to his cake. After a silence he gave the newspaper on the coffee table a slap. "Look at this. Flesh-eating bacteria."

"Ah! Isn't that awful?" Jackie said. Her blue eyes swept them all.

"Some people say it's been brought into the country," Arne said. He set down his plate and drew himself up in the chair. "They think it's part of a lot bigger thing."

"I wonder." Jackie turned her large dazed eyes full onto Arne. Gradually her face emptied of the sweetness lying in the eggshell tints of the skin; it furrowed, took on concentration. "You know, Mr. Olson," she said, "May has told me about you." She studied him. "You're a police officer."

"I'm the one," Arne said.

May always made an effort to be like her daughters, who insisted on going to the door and flinging it open to let the subject of Nick in, but she was too tired, she didn't feel like going along, if Laura allowed the afternoon to take this turn.

"You're the one who tried to save May's son," Jackie went on relentlessly.

Arne's tan had darkened, mottled. He cleared his throat. "No. No, that's not the way I'd put it," he rasped. He looked at Laura for help, but Laura was cutting more cake. May couldn't help him; no one was going to help him. "I guess it's up to—" He jabbed his thumb at the ceiling.

"To God." Jackie gave him a long look over the edge of her cup. "You . . . have . . . religious faith," she said with deep sobriety.

"I wish that was true."

May closed her eyes and let her head fall back on the cushions. Was there a subtle, sneaking advantage to the weariness the stroke had left her? Into the past, even into the immediate past, even into Jackie's beauty, had crept this restful unimportance. She was beyond it. And was Arne, too, beyond this old ritual of theirs? No, you could hear in his voice that he wasn't. If anything it was stronger in him; he was waiting for the rounding off, the release into the next year.

Keeping her eyes closed, May began to breathe deeply and regularly. Sure enough, there was a pause during which she could hear Jackie rustling, gesturing to Arne: *she's going to sleep.*

"I don't have it, faith," Jackie said. "I just plain don't. I'm what you'd call an agnostic." She paused, assessing the effect of the word. But now she was not to be stopped, she was getting her teeth into the subject, with the strong sense she always had of what was important to a man. "It's probably wrong but I sort of feel that, for me, I might be looking for something that isn't in the files." No one else spoke. Was Laura in the room anymore? "You're pretty sure it isn't in there, actually, so that, I mean, should you start in on hours and hours of looking for it? When you're pretty sure it was never even there in the first place?"

"You're not sure it's *not* there." May heard Arne's cup rock in the saucer.

"What about some more cake?" Laura said. So she was in the room.

"But just say it isn't. Here, look." Jackie was tapping along the coffee table, it seemed, with the edge of a hand. May opened her eyes. *She's doing file folders,* she thought with a familiar glee, and closed them again. "Now," Jackie said, "it can be misfiled to kingdom come, if you know, if you have *proof* it's in there, you just keep looking, it's worth it. The same way it's worth it if you know you dropped your contact *in the bathroom*. You know it has to be *in that room*, somewhere near the sink. Do you see what I mean?"

Here May opened her eyes again to send Jackie a look—*Don't take anything away from Arne.* Arne was unclenching his big hand as if he had just punched somebody. But Jackie would know not to do that, remove any prop. Looking at the fist, the red face, she would know. And she did, she put her fingers up to her soft cheek and leaned forward politely as Arne said, "But wait a minute!"

"Religion," Laura put in unexpectedly, "is the sigh of the op-pressed creature. You always said that, Mom. Leaving out what *God* might be," she added soothingly, to Arne.

"*I* didn't say . . . no . . . I quoted . . . my mother."

"Her mother was a lapsed Catholic," Laura explained to Jackie.

"I can go with that," Arne said.

"Oh, I agree," Jackie cried, posing her head so that she ap-peared to be looking up, like Princess Di. A familiar look. May could place it, a look from below you on the steps. She had seen the same look when her sister Carrie greeted Laban, the young minister, and made it her business to marry him. May happened to know that Jackie had toyed with Scientology, and after that the Foursquare Church. *Agnostic!* Jackie! What was the word for a person who was ready to believe anything?

Arne was leaning over the table dipping his cake into his cof-fee, his neck sunk between his shoulders. "How's this?" He took a deep breath, expanding the shirt May knew he had ironed himself, and blew it out. "Sigh of the oppressed creature," he said, looking around brightly. Jackie laughed, and gave a musical sigh of her own. Arne had set his legs squarely apart so that the trousers, pulled tight, had to be loosened from the bunched muscles of his thighs.

"Not today," he said to Jackie, with a broadly signifying look at May, "but I'll tell you the whole thing some time."

Arne had had two wives already, he was halfway down the road to being crazy, he gambled away everything he had, he was too old for Jackie. But maybe not.

For as long as he lived, Cole thought of Arne as the person who killed Nick. May could not remember when she had realized this. She sometimes wished she had heard him say it, encouraged him in some way to speak his mind about Arne, but he had stopped short of that. May suspected that it was for Laura's sake that he had refrained. They were careful with Laura. Laura had been thirteen when Nick was born, the kind of sister who was half mother. When Nick died, her way back was as slow as the arrow that never arrived because the distance it was traveling could still be cut in half.

It was not that Laura was a pushover. It was not as if Arne Olafsson would come out a hero, if Laura were to tell it. She would simply be factual, chronological, as she had been in her books: Arne didn't leave the city, he didn't leave his job. Despite the fact that he wasn't going anywhere on the force, he stayed. The department didn't get rid of him but it was clear he was being kept on and that was all. He didn't seem to care. As a cop it was no use to have ambition anyway, once you got the label *oddball*. He had had his event, and gone inside it, and his loyalty was to it.

Arne's hair went white, in stark contrast to the tan he got from the hours he spent on a tanning bed, cultivating an orangey tea color year-round, which everyone else found comical. He told May about the comments he got at the station; he was one of those people who don't know any better than to tell stories on themselves. But he didn't start drinking, and he was proud of that. He did lose his wife, and then his second wife, the one who got to be a friend of May's. Missing a rung here and there, with a momentary jolt, and then catching itself, getting its balance, his life went in little stumbles downward. He started to gamble. Just poker at first, he told May. "Hey, I'm watching it." Then the gambling got a little out of control, and he lost his house.

He felt less guilty about that than May would have supposed, all of his guilt being taken up elsewhere. About the gambling he seemed content with a kind of bashful, sentimental regret, as May discovered when she took a ride with him in his patrol car. "Listen to this," he said, putting in a tape. He wanted her to hear a bluegrass song about a gambling man whose mother kept sending him warnings from the back of a playing card. "That gets me," he said, driving with his eyes on the rearview mirror, as was his habit.

Around the fifth year, Arne said to May, "I have something to tell you." This was soon after he married his second wife, Lorraine, when the house they were living in was being sold out from under them. "I've accepted Jesus Christ."

"I'm glad. I always wish I knew what that *is*. What's involved."

"You just . . . you see how things could be different. From here on out I feel like I can quit dwelling on it."

"How things could be different. That's good."

"I don't know." He scratched his tanned neck.

"It's good."

"Well, to tell the truth, I'm not as convinced as Lorraine. But she's had the Lord a lot longer. She knows this stuff."

After their divorce this second wife did not abandon Arne. Months before he told May about it, Lorraine had called her to say, "I thought you ought to know we're separating."

"Thanks for calling me," May said. "Oh, what's going to happen to him?"

"I'll keep in contact," Lorraine said. Contact. A word May had not let her students use, as verb or noun. But Lorraine's heart was in the right place. "Anymore, I feel like he'll stay where he is now," she said. "I don't feel like I was for a while, that he'll go down. But you know him. He's got it on his conscience. You know the problem."

"I think so," May said. At one time she would have pursued this line of talk so that she could give her version, in which everything that led up to that particular night was carefully pieced in and basted together into a plausible whole. This attempt led her on a path to hidden, guarded stores of blame. Self-blame, for the most part, but also blame of others who would never suspect they were even involved. Girlfriends, teachers, doctors. She held on to it, made it precious for a while, if for no other reason than to fight off the articles and books forbidding blame, which her friends sent her. She no longer prized this version, with the luxury of blame and possible punishment. Next she resumed the piecing together and the retelling, and the process grew so exhaustive and complicated that everyone got off, more or less; they all jumped ship one by one, on a rope of details, leaving Nick to go down alone. She no longer covered that ground either. Words could not come anywhere near the pulsing, living, enshrined truth.

"I can't blame Lorraine, she wants kids," Arne said, about his divorce. It seemed he shot blanks. That was how he put it.

But Lorraine was a decent person. She had to be, as Arne pointed out; she had no choice, she had the Lord. The mysterious Lord. On that subject May was cautious. After all these years she still felt an undertow from anybody who had that particular settled, satisfied attitude, like a person after a big Thanksgiving dinner. Anybody decent, that is. Anybody happy. Had there been a time when she could have gone in that direction? She had longed for someone, after all. No one she knew, no one human. She had petitioned someone in secret, those first years, to take hold of her and wring out the dark water and bring her back. Rescue her.

Was it the Lord who gave Lorraine a new husband and two sons? Lorraine was the kind of woman who sent out oversize pop-up cards announcing IT'S A BOY! May had hers on the mantel for so long the second one appeared beside it.

"I thought about whether I oughta send you that announcement," Lorraine said the first time, hoisting the baby in his plastic carrier. "You know." She and May were halfway to being friends by then.

How many people all over the world believed a son to be the gift tumbled most directly from the hand of God? Why did they believe that—women consulting doctors, climbing up temple steps in supplication? But May was getting away from the chronology, putting in her stubborn questions and opinions. Opinion: that was what Laura would leave out if she were to write the story.

Whoever or whatever provided Lorraine with her conviction, May thought, in the long run she deserved its rewards, for her loyalty. Half the time she and her husband paid Arne's rent, as he went on gambling, flying to Reno on weekends. "It isn't money, it's luck. It's *chance*. That's what has the guy by the balls," Lorraine said.

At Arne's wedding May had to meet many members of his family, with whom she pretended her speech was worse than it really was. She had fallen into this restful disguise on more than one occasion. The family had assembled dutifully for Arne's third wedding. It was held in Lorraine's church because neither Arne nor Jackie had one. The parking lot was filled with squad cars, and an officer's radio squawked and called him out in the middle of the vows. None of this deterred Lorraine's minister, who conducted a brisk, smiling ceremony, during which Jackie's boy and girl, in two thin, true strands of soprano, sang "You Light Up My Life," and Arne became so lightheaded with emotion that he had to lean on the bride's arm.

Jackie wore a full-scale wedding dress, as people did now for second and third weddings, and many in the church, not just May, got out their handkerchiefs when she appeared in the wide doorway with her father—who had had to be discouraged from wearing the button his lodge had given him saying "This is the last time I'll do this"—and walked down the aisle with the stately, slightly tottering bride's walk she had always had.

Among the guests was Jackie's grandmother. She was May's age, and drank so much champagne it looked by the end of the evening as if she and not May had had the stroke.

The reception went on and on because none of the cops would

go home, and Jackie and Arne weren't going anywhere because they had the kids with them; they were going home to Jackie's house, where they had been living since the week they met.

Lorraine had more of a sense than the first wife of what had happened to Arne. She saw him as having been removed from the normal course of events, having a different row to hoe, as she put it. She saw him as the penitent he was. That was it.

She had always gone to some pains to observe Arne's birthday, and when he got diabetes, even though it was mild at first, she was the one who made sure he had the kit and stuck himself in the finger and kept a log of his blood sugar. She kept track, she kept in contact, she did it for years.

At Arne's funeral, May sat between Lorraine and Jackie, who occasionally leaned forward to smile at each other across her, through their tears. Lorraine's church was being remodeled, so the funeral was held in an old Catholic church that now belonged to charismatics; they had removed the statues from their niches but took advantage of the kneelers. Jackie's two children sang "He Will Raise You Up on Eagle's Wings," taught to them in one day by Lorraine.

Lorraine and Jackie stayed in the pew and each put an arm around May when everybody knelt down to receive the long and somehow extenuating benediction called down on them by the same cheerful man who had performed the marriage.

Laura and Vera were both overseas. From the nursing home where she had gone to live after her second stroke, May came with an attendant. By that time she really couldn't talk, though her eyes could show her admiration for Lorraine's growing boys, and she could take satisfaction in a bear hug from Lorraine's husband, who was fatter now than Arne had been. She pressed Lorraine's hand to her cheek as firmly as she could. She comforted Jackie—married and made a widow in a year, but if she could, May would have said to the tearstained Lorraine, *You are the real widow.*

To all of them she presented the attendant who had accompanied her from the nursing home, a tall, shy, sweet-natured boy named Sven.

Sitting in the pew she came to the conclusion that even when he got the Lord, Arne had not seen how things could be different, after all. He had said he did but he didn't. He must have seen that things could not be different. Lay the cards down, lay them face down. They must be as they are.

That was how Laura might tell it.

Going to See the Bees: Sven

This was the day, and it whistled and snapped with the appetites of the first starlings. Before the sun cast any light in the room May woke up to the sound of the birds, and a voice she had been hearing in her dream.

"Dohn do it. Dohn do it."

It was Renee, her soft Haitian English. And unmistakably, Sven's voice. "Gotta do it, I swear to God it's OK."

Then both sinking to whispers, and Renee's rising again in a moan. "No . . . dohn do it for them . . . I'm beg . . . they cahn make you . . ."

May had just gone back to sleep from lying awake in the middle of the night while Mr. Dempsey was being taken away. She didn't have to guess, she knew whose room, astir with hushed effort and the balking wheels of the gurney, had slid the light under her door, though of course there was no sound from Dempsey to say whether he lived or died. Then she had fallen into a fitful sleep in which she was driving the car while pulling another car with a rope, keeping it alongside the one she was driving, with her arm bent uncomfortably out the window. Renee was somewhere out of sight, sadly, falteringly urging her, "Dohn do it."

This was to be the day of the trip to see the bees. They were taking a ferry to the Olympic Peninsula, to a farm as pretty as anything you would ever see, said Charlotte, the day supervisor. Her brother-in-law was the farmer and beekeeper. Charlotte's opinions could be off by many degrees. Still, the hope was born.

Sven was driving and there was plenty of room for Renee in the huge new van—a bus, this one was—but the supervisor had the say. "No matter her, I will take Jean-Baptiste for new shoes," Renee said proudly when she got the news, with a look that was peculiarly hers, half bitterness, half surrender, as she opened the sleeve for May to put her arm in. But Renee was not stoical, her eyes slid to May's calendar with its circled date, the date of going to see the bees, and she blurted something in French. A curse, May thought, though Renee's fingers stayed light on her buttonholes.

May had yet to fasten her own buttons. Sleep still caught her in her chair or else moved out of reach for a week at a time, but she could talk a little now. Words took shape, to be guessed at by the others.

May held a position of her own, as most of them did. Knitter, Bible reader, cardsharp. May was *Sven's favorite*. They all said she was, and privately she thought so too. No reason for it, but it had happened before; she had had students like Sven. Strays, uncoachable ballplayers, thin drifting boys too old for the class they were in, who conferred on her somewhere in the middle of the school year a half-surprised liking. At first Sven's partiality had stirred up some ill will, but that had faded once it was clear May was not especially lucky otherwise, not the youngest or the soundest of them by any means, though not the worst off, either.

One or two had been there years, back to Reagan. She knew that from the angry, quavering political arguments that sometimes broke out in a little circle of the men. Two against two, two patchily shaved old men she called the CEOs, against the sawmill foreman trying to catch his spit and pointing with a stub of finger, and the new man, who had been a minister, Mr. Tower. Already May was not the most recent; she had been there since the first week of the dark New Year, the same day the carpenters got there.

The center was outsourcing rehab; where rehab had been, there would soon be a full-care wing with its own lounge. May had heard it from Charlotte. A private group had taken over rehab, and now they traveled four blocks in the van to a building with dentists' offices and a ground-level suite labeled AMBULA-TION AND FINE MOTOR.

So, in some minds, added to the attention from Sven which she had to answer for, other changes too had come with May's arrival: weeks of saws whining and plaster dust in the food, and sharp paint fumes making their eyes run. But she had managed it, eased her walker up and down the ramps a hundred times and then lost count, torn up the furious unmailed scrawls—"Can't feel my arm"—to her daughter Laura.

If she had complained, Laura would have come from overseas and taken her back with her. Given an opening, she would do it now. Vera would fly in too, and they would pack her up and hand her over to the household of her son-in-law. For really that was what it was: Will's big shady house in a suburb of Kuala Lumpur, where Laura lived calmly. As May could not, in Will's dominion. No, she could not. Nevertheless they would have their way, lift her out of the waters that were hers: the rain, the Sound, the snow-fed rivers, the lake where her child had died. There would be no way to stand up to the three of them.

No one would promise another stroke was not coming to finish her off. Or worse, not finish her. But for the time being she was holding her own. The walker had given way to a four-pronged aluminum cane with a wrist strap. Not long after that she had tackled stairs. Two, four, and finally six times a day she had practiced with a bored aide, and now they were letting her go up and down by herself. She had her place now.

And at last the sun had made it, a slim bright edge to the blinds every morning, with ladders clanking as the work moved outdoors, and a rain of pinfeathers from the routed starlings. Day after day she saw the birds waiting it out in the trees, eyeing the gutters and eaves as if their own numbers, their persistence, were known to them.

Warmed out of sloth, May revived; they all did. In the lounge they dragged their chairs in a gradual circle, following the sun, a few women who never got dressed running splinters into their heels in the no-slip socks. Even the face of the haunted Mr. Dempsey, who had lost all language, could be seen tilted to the sun with the right eye half closed.

Dempsey had been an early, ghostly friend to May. From the first day, she looked straight into the mutant grin he could wring from his cheek muscles but not get rid of. It took him five minutes to iron out the dimple under the cheekbone. Both hands dangled at his crotch, but eventually he managed to heave his torso against the wheelchair strap and reach out as May passed to dab her buttocks with the good hand.

His wordlessness had the appearance of consent, even choice; he did not cheat it by making so much as a sound. The drooping lid gave him a sagacious, carnal, forecasting look.

Dempsey had a son. A rich lawyer, Renee said. The son visited weekly, sometimes more, embracing him each time with shameless tears. The daughter-in-law came too, often with fudge, or a pie she would cut for him on the spot and share around the lounge. May noticed that for this woman Dempsey strained himself dark red to produce the grin.

A man with a sweet tooth, and a weakness for women. Dempsey had been a union official, May knew that much, a longshoreman. In her mind she took to carrying on with him the conversation they would have had—or she thought so anyway—about the two old reactionaries in the lounge, the CEOs. *Listen to them,* she said to Dempsey in her mind. *What are they doing here if it's every man for himself?*

A painter had crouched for two days blowing off starling feathers and putting the new logo for the Center for Extended Care on signs and doors, and on the huge van, "CEC" in gold script with flourishes. To herself May pronounced it "Sick." She made an effort to print her idea on a pad for Dempsey; there was no way he could tell what she was getting at but at least he smiled his canny smile. In the big new van, a dozen people could fit, in seatbelts, but fewer than that usually went. Four or five would go to church, six or seven to the mall. For special outings it was said they would have to draw straws, but May couldn't see where such numbers would come from. The walkers and canes went into a well in the back. As many as three wheelchairs could go, collapsed by Sven.

The decision was Charlotte's, and she liked to keep outings small. Even if they were to draw straws, Charlotte would make some final calculation. Her morning duties meant she had to come after them on a later ferry, bringing the picnic and a canvas bag bulging with the map game, packs of cards, and the drawing game no one would play.

Charlotte was often in a girlish huff but never hostile—you had to give her that, May thought. She was always in a state of fellowship, if anyone would respond when she rounded them up for Trivial Pursuit, or wolf-whistled after the men she was logging out to PT on her clipboard. Sometimes she stepped into the bathroom with one of her sign-up sheets while Renee was washing someone. At fifty Charlotte was the size of a sixth-grade girl; standing straight in heels she came up to Renee's shoulder. She had been grooming Renee for more responsibility until the affair with Sven came to light. Charlotte would have the say. Whose turn was it? With a full staff there for the day, and an extra car going, there was no reason Renee and her little son couldn't go too, but it wasn't Renee's turn.

To make up for it, the week before the trip Charlotte was friendlier than usual and tracked Renee down more than once in order to ask her spirited questions about Haiti. Not about what they saw in the papers, refugees drowning or Aristide or the present situation at all, but voodoo, and "those old dictators, those Papas."

"I dohn know," Renee murmured. Or she merely smiled and shrugged.

Once May knew she would be one of those going on the excursion, she dragged out volumes of the old *Collier's* encyclopedia in the lounge. When she began to read, laboriously, it was all familiar from her students' papers. Bees, the Human Eye, the Greek Myths. Hinduism, the Ku Klux Klan: she could vault down the alphabet of their favorites.

She studied the head-on enlargement of the worker bee's face, the giant badge eyes, blind-looking, innocent. Poor hunched compelled undesiring female. No student had written about that, the sadness of the facial configuration of the bee. Bavaria, Behaviorism, Black Death. If she shut her eyes she could almost feel the school around her. The library's humming fluorescent lights, the PA system. "First-period English, meet your rides in the parking lot." The Ford station wagon she had held on to year after year for field trips.

Where was her car? Did she still own it?

That was something it did not pay to think about. The car. Herself at the wheel, on the way to plays and games, contests, the library downtown. Kids yelling and singing, the time in the car being the seriously anticipated part of the trip. All of them changing a tire beside the freeway. She had taught each of her children to drive, and the girls had been good drivers. Nick . . . for him the near-aliveness of a car, the force showing itself as obedience, had had to be tested. But she wouldn't think about Nick either. She kept recollection to a minimum. Twenty years had taught her to sense the approach of a given scene by its aura, and to stop the drift toward certain occasions of the past. Almost always, if they stirred in their fog she turned her back.

When she couldn't sleep, and without meaning to—foolish to begin planning in advance—she had put together a scenario for the visit to the beehives, and refined and embellished it until finally it produced the guilty satisfaction of a scene she might find herself gazing at in the art booths people set up now in the middle of the mall. One of those oils with no brushstrokes, propped on an easel. A field of high grass washing back and forth, here and there laid down like a rack of dresses. The group of them wading diagonally into the picture, leaving a deep track, May somehow having a wide, convex view of them from behind and above, and of a field with orchards in flower on two sides, though it was summer and not spring. The field having dropped steeply off, the whole dark blue Sound stretched itself before them. At the same time May was able to sweep the grassheads and the yellow and lavender weeds with her arms, and retie a straw hat around her damp neck, on her way to the village of white boxes in a shady corner of the field. The beehives.

It would be . . . glorious. Even Charlotte would recognize that it was glorious, and she would let them—let them what?

No. More likely after the ferry ride and the drive they would pull up in front of a house, a tidy rambler with pinwheels in the yard, a Charlotte's-sister kind of house. Climb down from the van on Sven's arm. Limp around back to beehives lined up along an electrified fence keeping a pen of steers with drugged eyes out of the hobby orchard.

And the brother-in-law would lecture them just like the Discovery Channel about the habits of bees—industrious females and short-lived males, the signaling dance in the air, and all the furious instinctive packed-in group existence. All that. But not let them come close to see for themselves, for fear of liability, while instead of the hot dogs being briskly grilled by Charlotte's sister, they would eat sandwiches marked by the dietitian with their names. But this was not the way to think about it, either, May told herself, any more than the first.

In fact the keeper of the bees might be a good-natured, oppressed fellow—married to a sister of Charlotte's, after all—full of sad restraint, who saw from the beginning that they required nothing more of this outing than the view from the ferry deck and then two picnic tables and a jar of honey. But chewing his hot dog he would catch May's eye, he would wink, stroll over to her where she sat, and invite her, and Sven with her, to ride on the old tractor with him. It would be Sven's style to jump on, whatever Charlotte hollered at him. And then in some configuration allowing two to stand on the tractor with the poise of charioteers, out of reach of the great tires, the three of them would ride to the back of the orchard, through which a creek would be winding half buried in grass, to an old grove of lightning-killed trees where the escaped swarm, with the old queen who had banished herself, had their own kingdom, their queendom.

So May had imagined the visit to the beehives, in her room at the center with her eyes open in the green light of the digital clock.

Awake at all hours and pushing at the night where she lay under its intimate weight, she had made a kind of discovery, of the reverse of night, the obvious open *day,* and grown childishly possessive of it—the faithfully arriving unsingular daytime, into whose current she had swung her bare feet so many thousands of times. How she had been fooled, fooled into nonchalance by its familiarity! She of all people—whose students had joked about her making them read books so familiar by title that they believed they had already read them. "Sure I read *Huckleberry Finn,*" they always said, juniors in high school. "Way back when."

What was it about?

"Oh, you know. Tom Sawyer?"—this was a joke. She laughed at their jokes, which went on all year until the time came at the end of her course when they were finished with the memoirs she had Xeroxed for them to read, and sat down to write their own autobiographies.

"You can be funny," she urged them. "I know somebody in this class has had something funny happen." But humor had fled, when they wrote down what they considered, at that moment, to be their lives. Half of them wrote as if she had made a rule that they break her heart. And that was as good a rule as any in autobiography class, was it not? Though she had not, of course, made that rule.

If Sven was a loose cannon who considered himself above the rules, still, May thought, he had natural politeness with his elders. Though if there were parents, they were somewhere far back—Sven was skin and bones, he had no money—and if she thought about it she couldn't really see a father at all. Sven didn't talk sports with Shawn and Rafael, the other male aides, or take his break with them. All three satisfied themselves with "How's it goin'?" Renee confirmed it. "No fahmily," she told May, shaking her head as you would over something hatched out with one leg.

Renee had made the mistake of trying to give Sven presents, shirts and even shoes. The shoes did it. May heard him: "So take them back!"

"So I will take them, but why cahn you wear them this one hour?" They were going to her niece's first communion.

"Like I give a shit?" This provoked in Renee a little startled sob. "Hey! Not about church, hey, I want to go. Look, the shoes are great. Thank you! I mean it. Just—*I'll* buy shoes, all right?" But once, Renee had on earrings she told May Sven had bought her, and they were gold. They flashed aggressively at the corners of her smooth jaw, the kind of big flashy earrings a little boy might want to buy his mother.

Sven was used to being alone, May could see that in the way he watched over himself, feeling his way. Except with women: the female aides and the receptionist and the dietitian, even Charlotte. With women he had a casual boldness.

He played the bass guitar in a rock group. His mind wasn't on his job because he was trying to *make it,* Charlotte said. They were lucky he didn't come to work in the stuff he wore to perform. "How does she know?" Frieda snorted, clashing her knitting needles. Frieda lived in the room next to May's, and liked to poke a needle in Charlotte's direction when her back was turned.

It was quite possible to imagine Charlotte buying a ticket and stationing herself—frosted hair, blazer, pleated skirt—in the crowd at the base of the stage. Snapping her fingers, wearing her expectant look, her bright, lost, cinematic smile. Before she came here, but how long ago she wasn't sure, May had seen bodies on TV being tossed up and passed along to music, some graceful, rising and traveling like mermaids above the crowd, some all elbows and flailing legs. The mermaids rolled along on a fin of arms, the clumsy ones scrambled and thrashed and even tried to stand up, and toppled back to be sucked into the crowd upside down. Here and there the crowd-surfing might still get started, more of a joke now, at the end of a long night when people were pretty high, Sven told her. If it did, he liked to get into it. Just as in the old days, it could go on relatively peacefully for some time. Sometimes it got out of control. She could see on his arms, below the black and green of his tattoo, the big purple fingerprints.

One Monday out of three Sven might fail to show up for work, but when he supervised an outing he did the job he had been hired to do. In winter he would hand each one of them down the van's high step—now with the new bus, there were three steps—sheltering them with an umbrella until they were all gathered under the awning, and then hold the heavy doors of the Bon Marché while they filed in. He took care of details but he was attending to his own business at the same time. He was waiting for something. Sometimes he whistled softly, and wrote something down on a scrap of paper. Sometimes if a voice surprised him, he ducked.

May could not help picturing Sven as a child, told to wait, left in charge of something, and keeping at it for hours, days, only gradually discovering himself forsaken.

"Look at me when I'm talking to you, Sven!" Charlotte would pout, a brownish rose color spreading over her small face, dug out under the eyes and soft-skinned with estrogen.

But May had caught Sven actually looking at her, and at the others in the center, with fixed, acknowledging eyes. She didn't know whether to be gratified or ashamed.

Sven would go back cheerfully for handbags and pills, and get out the paper cups he kept in the glove compartment so they could have a drink of water. Mr. Dempsey would show he wanted his forelock combed back out of his eyes or he would jiggle his shoe to get Sven to close the Velcro tabs. When Sven came back from parking the van, most of them would go some way into the mall and settle on the benches.

Sometimes he would bring them coffee and then disappear into the CD store. The twins, Nita and Nalda, in their schoolgirl mood of perpetual recess, would press May to say what she was thinking. The knowledge that she had taught school led to the idea that she was always thinking. And that had to do with Sven, didn't it? Didn't it?

The twins had picked up, by some means other than their rote questions, a signal of the liking that had sprung up between Sven and May. They were not jealous; they enlarged their infatuation to include her. She could not pass their door without the blessing of their causeless, eager laughter. They slipped notes under her door, and dashed half-dressed out of their room across the hall to tiptoe after her in their knee-highs, slip straps down their puckered arms, teasing for her notice.

In the mall, they spied on Sven as he talked on the phone, each with a crooked finger in the air for silence. Sometimes Sven would be making calls the whole time he was keeping watch over them, holding the phone to his ear with his shoulder.

May could close her eyes and bring on a dreamy, river-floating sensation: footsteps, creaking strollers, brightness on all sides, espresso vapor in the air, throbs from the CD store coming through the soles of her Nikes, though the numb foot could only believe what the other one reported—all of it muffled as if the two strokes had encased her in fur, and all having to be sorted and identified.

Unless she had a mirror it was not a sure thing her hand would find her hair, or her scalp know her hand had found it. She could not be sure the hair was in the comb. Everything took sorting.

One of the twins would say, "Sven called up Renee, I know he did!" In the cafeteria, or beached in the lounge while grade-schoolers sang to them, or on the new grass where a few would sit in deck chairs now, the twins never tired of the subject of Sven and Renee. All day, when they weren't napping in their seats, they would gossip and invent. But phone calls between Sven and Renee, or kisses sneaked in Clean Utility, took the twins just as far, May decided, as they liked to go; beyond that lay a world barely remembered, and unregretted.

May herself did not add to the gossip, though she had witnessed more than kisses, but she couldn't help listening to it, or studying the chemical blue of Sven's eyes under the ledge of forehead, his thin-edged nostrils, his flat fingers silvery with calluses from pulling the fat bass strings. May was curious about his music and she knew that was one reason he liked her.

She liked him a great deal now, since she had seen him naked. On Mr. Dempsey's stripped bed, with Renee. May had not said good-bye to Mr. Dempsey that morning, the first time they took him back to the hospital. He had passed out in the lounge. She hadn't shaken his paper-skinned hand or wished him luck before they rolled him out, or indeed heard about it at all until hours later, and she was worrying about him, talking to herself.

Mr. Dempsey, I hope you will not give up just yet.

She meant to let herself into Dempsey's room to hide his magazine collection from Charlotte. She heard a sound before she saw the two on the bed. As she backed out, stabbing her bad toenail with the cane, she was sure she had seen in Sven's unhumiliated look at her, with his long hands protectively around Renee's face, the steady man he was going to be.

"Don't worry, it was just May." She heard that.

Sven never mentioned it, of course. That week he played her a tape of one of his songs, though. He came in with a cassette player. "It's a ballad, more or less," he said, actually reddening as he pushed the button. The vocalist, who was not Sven, sang in a high, agonized register, and on one hearing May could make out only a few of the words. She heard "suck," though the song seemed less about sex than some hateful, unshakable obligation. Played differently the tune would have been pretty and sad. She could hear the steady pulse of the bass, and runs that lifted off with a casual trickiness from the rhythmic, laboring grunt. She said, "Good, good." It *was* good, she suspected.

She knew that in addition to the bass guitar, Sven played the upright bass, keyboard, harmonica, and sometimes, though he could not read music, the cello. The one he borrowed to play, he told her, was a cello neck without a body, plugged into an amp. Still, you played with a bow, you were playing the cello. Sometimes he bowed the upright bass. That was his favorite instrument, he said, and he had worked it into core songs for the CD. On the bulletin board in the reception area there was a picture of him cradling it. It had taken him years to pay for this bass, which was old and scratched.

May always took credit privately for predicting the romance between Sven and Renee. She had watched it begin, the looks, the loud jokes between them getting softer and less frequent, like birdsong thinning out in the morning as the birds get down to business. Sven was a secretive boy but he let her see it, she realized, long before the bedroom incident. Regardless of her loose arm and wet lip, he had taken the word of her daughter about her. "She understands everything. Don't forget, she knows." Her sensible Laura, turning in circles and repeating herself to Sven all afternoon, the day May moved in, because he was the one bringing in suitcases and plants and books, getting May settled. The day before, Laura and Will had come with a U-Haul, and put down the old Persian rug from the front hall and arranged May's dresser and whatever else would fit in the room. There was space for her own double bed but for a time she would have to sleep in a hospital bed with sides.

Later May was proud of herself for noticing, in her confusion on that occasion, some deftness or economy in what Sven was doing. It was in his hands as he set things on her shelves and her dresser. "I know you'll want to rearrange this," he said apologetically, while she sat by in the new armchair Laura had bought. Was it comfortable? She did not know. She did not know. It was January. She knew that.

"Your daughters?" On the dresser he had placed her studio portrait of the two girls, and the yearbook picture of Nick. She nodded. "Your son?" He didn't hold it up for her to look at, as he had the other one. She nodded again. She knew the nod was different and so, it seemed, did he. It seemed he knew, as he looked at the picture and back at her, that Nick was dead.

Laura was gone. The lamp was off—May had done that herself, practicing with the ingenious string arrangement swiftly demonstrated by Sven. She was waiting for dinner, which would be eaten at five. Laura had said as she kissed her that Sven would be there to take her to the dining room. Already she could smell the food, a gravy smell. Her first dinner. Laura had wanted to stay, but someone—had this been Charlotte?—had said no, not the first meal. "She'll be meeting her table. Come back tomorrow and you'll see it went just fine." So Laura was coming back in the morning.

When May turned her head she saw a tall thin boy with sunken eyes, and behind him someone else. She jumped. "Oh, dear, on the first day I see a ghost," she said to Sven—to herself, of course, because at that point she never could have produced that many words, and was she now a woman who would begin every sentence "Oh, dear," if she could talk? And it was only the young man's thin back, and his white-blond ponytail in the dimness of the dresser mirror, in this room where she would be living. *I thought I saw my son.*

A few days later Sven gave her a pad of paper. "You write for me. Then you fold the paper. Then you stick it in my shirt pocket, see, like this. Here, I'll button it and you unbutton it. Use that hand."

"Franklin H. S." She printed it laboriously.

He wanted her to use the right hand that wouldn't obey, but he praised her for the left-handed printing. He studied the scratches on the paper and said, "You were a teacher, I know that." She grasped the pencil and drew a question mark. "You mean me? No, I didn't go to Franklin. I look familiar? Nope, no brothers, no sisters." *Nobody,* she thought. "I look familiar to everybody," he added pleasantly. Right away she noticed the pleasantness.

If she could have said, "I don't know why that would be," she would have, because he did not look familiar to her at all, really, with that thin wolfish face, only partly softened by the fair hair. Something had told him to give her the pad and she wanted to write on it to establish herself.

He went to work on her speech, making her talk. When his shift didn't match Renee's, he gave May messages for Renee. "Tell her, 'Anytime.'" This was said in a tone that surprised May, both harsh and intimate, with the blue eyes narrow. But then sweetly to May, "Lemme hear you say it. Come on." And later, "Tell her yeah, no problem, bring the kid. I mean 'yes.' Say the *s*." He told her, "This place used to have a speech therapist. Real good guy. Over in rehab."

"Wha—"

"*Whatt*—form your lips—*whatt—happened.*"

"Wha—happuh?"

"Well, I'll tell ya. In these outfits, they get rid of the ones who know what they're doing. I know. I'm what you might call a veteran of rehab. Anybody tell you that? No? Old Charlotte didn't? Well, you can handle it, right? You tell Renee, 'He told me all about *rehab.*'" Sven's snicker jolted May back to the classroom. He had that high-pitched, two-second laugh of boys made to shut up at home.

Renee's voice was deeper than Sven's and she was his height, six feet. But she was stronger than he was. He had cords of muscle in the forearm from dragging on the strings of the upright bass, but he couldn't pick Mr. Dempsey up out of the chair the way Renee did. Smiling, she told May of her brother with AIDS in Port-au-Prince, and her sister Annette here, mother of the niece who was having her first communion when Renee bought Sven the shoes. Annette was unemployed and took care of Renee's son. She had to be called several times a day, from the phone in May's room—checked on and reminded and sometimes threatened. In addition, Renee had an ex-husband who siphoned off some of the paycheck with which she supported her son, her sister, her niece, and her mother. Renee had paid her mother's way from Haiti. Like May, her mother had had a stroke, and she lived sitting in a chair in Annette's apartment waiting for Renee. But unlike May she was young; Renee was thirty-one, her mother forty-six. "Very bad, now." Renee showed May a picture of her mother as she had been, a laughing woman with shiny black skin and tied-up hair, throwing out grain to chickens.

"Home . . . home . . ." May began.

"Hohm-sick." Renee nodded, closing her eyes and deeply wrinkling her brow at the same time her cheeks curved high with her broad, all-meaning smile. Her face had a contained light like that in aluminum, but the smoothness of her skin was not absolute; there were scuffed patches May noticed with some relief, at the elbows and knees, and behind the knee, soft bluish knots Renee had shown her in the bathroom when she first bared her own legs with the spider veins.

In the early morning May listened for Renee's *"Bonjour!"* as she passed from room to room, still in her guard's uniform, dropping the aluminum sidebars some of them had on their beds.

Renee had a night job as a security guard and she carried her weapon with her into the center rather than leave it in the car. She unloaded it and when Charlotte was not around she gave one or two of the men a chance to look at it and weigh it in their hands. Three mornings a week she hung up the khaki uniform and stowed the holster in the staff lounge closet.

She guarded a music store not far from the mall. Bundling sheets into damp drifts in the hallway, she told May about shoplifters, the boy chased out of the stockroom at midnight, the junkie couple who pitched a tent behind the store, rolling it up in the early morning and hiding it behind the Dumpster. On one side of the store there was a unit for rent and on the other a building for sale, that was how they could get away with it. The man played the guitar, and once despite his filthiness he asked Renee to let him come into the store to try out an instrument. Did she do it? "Wohn hurt, if he wash his hands." So Renee let them both wash in the bathroom. Eyes downcast she smiled, slowly closing her lips over her big even teeth. Renee was part of the music world, in a way. When he stripped the cellophane off his new CDs, Sven wanted her opinion. "Hey. Check out the drummer."

Sven had dropped out of high school to write songs and play with his band, but he had his GED and he was smart, he could sit in for the receptionist at the computer. He had shown May the lyrics to a number of his songs now; they were simple and harsh but there were no misspellings. Despite all the sex it seemed to May they had to do with something adverse, treacherous, and yet longed for, which might be drugs but might just as easily be the families they had all once had, or not had, or fame, or even God.

On paper the lines seemed vaguer and less anguished than she remembered hearing on the tape, but she decided to ask him nevertheless. One of these days she would print on her pad, *What's wrong?* Sometimes, with a student, that had been enough. If not, she knew to back off. On the other hand, how much had they ever said—the ones like Sven? They had sometimes seemed to her in her own classroom, sprawled at their desks asleep, to be like the boys in one of the memoirs she Xeroxed and handed out year after year: little boys in their country's army, being sent down the gauntlet. Her students might have rap sheets, but in the classroom they would be likely to identify with authority. If she gave them a story to read about a sentry who left his post to pull a drowning man out of a river, they would say he should have stayed in the booth.

Sven's band performed in clubs and toured fairs and campuses. May did not know whether this was success, but Renee seemed to think it was. He was not going to be famous, though, Renee said, her black eyes, with their smudged irises, flicking a little the way they did when she was thinking. No, there was a lid on fame. All the fame that was coming to the city had come already, bringing with it enough trouble in the form of heroin to hold the rest of them for years. *I know about that,* May would have said. *Heroin was here a long time ago.*

Still, Sven had a following. Brash, tinny voices—if not very little girls, then those who drew attention to themselves, May thought, by sounding like little girls—asked for Sven at all hours on the answering machine. If they were sitting in the lounge they could hear the voices when the message tape ran. Once May heard, "What the fuck? We waited all night. Listen, fucker—" before the receptionist cut it off. A little-girl voice. She hoped Renee had not heard that.

But Renee was not jealous. Sven was the jealous one. He did not like it when her ex-husband came by. He always put his arms around her after the husband left pocketing his loan—a man for Sven to pity, not worry about, in May's opinion, though he was from Renee's own town in Haiti and bore a trace of her hand-some tired sweetness.

Once he had the little boy with him, Jean-Baptiste. Annette was "down," Renee said, twisting her mouth in the angry despair she reserved for mention of her sister. The boy had the body of a stick figure and black eyes out of proportion to his head, like the bee illustrations. He had the small, thin face of his father, dark skin stretched cheekbone to cheekbone as if with thumbs. He was four. Renee knelt down and kissed all along his hairline. Of course money had to be found, for something so small and pro-visional, half shadow, without a root in life at all, it seemed. The husband jingled his change and held the spidery little hand loosely in his. It was this that Sven was jealous of. It was for this he wanted money, to lure both mother and son, May thought. To best the slouching, grinning father.

"That man—he believe in that stuff," Renee told her. "That voodoo. His mother at home, she is *mambo*."

"But it's a religion like any other, isn't it? Just misunderstood," May heard her teacher voice begin in her head. Fortunately the voice was trapped and could not break out.

"That—spirits. Bad, bad," Renee said, making a chewing and spitting motion with her lips.

Mambo, May thought. *"Carrefour,"* she said clearly, surprising herself.

"Carrefour," Renee repeated, turning her mouth down but quickly adding, "That one, good some time, bad some time."

Carrefour. A rogue form of the good spirit, the *loa,* in Haiti. Carrefour used the split second between life and death to decide which way you would go.

When you were substituting, you might find yourself teaching any subject. In her days as a substitute May had taught math, geometry, chemistry. When the geography teacher had her baby early, May had made her way through a whole semester showing films: she patched together a tireless, fertile, randomly celebrating globe. Terraced farming. Festivals of the Andes. Dances of the Caribbean.

In Haiti the loa took possession of the dancer. The capricious, infernal Carrefour, guardian of the crossroads, was he one of those? Was he a god, whose decision could intervene in that last split second? There was no way to ask Renee, and anyway Renee's curved eyelids had dropped warningly, the way they did when Charlotte got going about Haiti.

Why did I always talk? May wondered. *I never just sat there like Renee does.* She felt a slow shock: what if all along there had been no need to speak?

The receptionist had chewed Sven out for that message on the machine. It was she who had tacked the picture of him to the bulletin board. May remembered jokes and threats between the girl and Sven in the winter, her pushing Sven out of the way with her hip as she dragged a cart of files backward into the office. Now she sulked in his presence or Renee's, and reminded him of some requirement of Charlotte's every time she handed him his schedule.

Sven brought in doughnuts the dietitian didn't allow and magazines that had to be hidden. For Mr. Dempsey he brought *Hustler,* and comics that came, Renee said, from a section of the comic store roped off for adults. Dempsey wrapped the magazines in his sweater or had Sven stuff them in the vinyl pocket of the wheelchair. To the twins Sven gave the *Enquirer* and *World.*

But of course Nita and Nalda did not read; their days were spent in sleep and spying and play. They were not interested in other people—even, or especially, their own families—they were interested in the people they saw every day, a few of them, and in themselves. Mostly in themselves, maybe because they found themselves mysteriously doubled again, May thought, after a life spent apart from each other with two different husbands.

There must have been the germ of hysteria in them as girls, May thought. They would have been twin hiders, pouncers, eggers-on, before the duties of marriage came between them. They had had their share of troubles, both of them, but those, Nita's daughter told Charlotte, had now been placed squarely in her, the daughter's, hands.

They were a pair of kites now, up in the sky with the string played all the way off the spool. They didn't look down to see their future in the Alzheimer's unit the carpenters were dry-walling now, in the wing where rehab had been. They had sailed out past their own lives.

Yet they and she, May learned one morning, were grouped to-gether in Charlotte's mind, classified: the laughers. Renee told her that. Renee was sitting on the bed shaving away at May's bad toenail with a razor blade. The nail had turned thick and yellow, and worked itself sideways into the toe so that it could not be cut. When she had finished with the nail Renee lifted May's legs over the side of the bed and dunked the foot in a plastic basin of hot suds. "Get that one, let her play too." May giggled, the dry foot obeyed.

Renee pointed at the twins' door. "So, you see? Like Charlotte say-s, you and them, laughers."

Thus May received Charlotte's judgment. "Not like them, you," Renee added quickly, glancing up. She patted May's toe with a cotton ball soaked in witch hazel, and began that lulling, pleas-antly deceitful singsong of hers. "You, now—pretty as Erzilie. Mm-hm. You know Erzilie? Pretty brown woman." She patted May's white hair. "*Très* smart. She like love." Renee smiled. "She come from the sea."

I'm not like those two, May said to herself. The twins had begun to slip mentally at about the same time, and been reunited here by Nita's daughter, after considerable upheaval in the two families when they ceased to bathe. May had eavesdropped more than once on the daughter as Charlotte talked to her: "She still sits on the edge of the tub and pretends, unless Renee's with her."

"Oh! She was *not like that,* believe me. Oh! She kept things so nice!"

"Well, don't you worry, we have her spic and span."

What did it matter, really, if you bathed or not?

But obviously it did matter, to people still in the world; it mattered when a woman smelled, it mattered when *matter* was involved and everybody's nose was being rubbed in it. Even here a humid, bacterial odor drifted from both twins if they sat by the radiator.

Or if it did not seriously matter whether you bathed, or whether you had the power of thought, what was it that did matter—if you were not a baby, of course, and were not to grow past this squalid idyll into a childhood?

What was the thing that mattered when nothing mattered?

"I ask this not out of discouragement," May began with some formality, addressing herself mentally as usual to the mismatched knowing eyes of Mr. Dempsey, "but in hopes of an answer. Now, in class I had to be careful not to answer my own question." And here she stopped, for what *did* she believe?

"Well, Dempsey won't be back this time." In the ferry snack bar Frieda sat tapping her hooked nails on the Formica. At the sound May felt her heart draw, like a glass going to the bottom of a dishpan. *"Wrong,"* she said angrily, but her knees began to knock under the table. She glared at Frieda, but that was what Frieda liked—attention.

With his hard fingers Sven was rubbing his eyebrows in circles against the large, overhung bone of his forehead, as if he had a headache. What was the matter with Sven?

He swung his long body out of the chair and away, his hair flashing yellow under the heat lamps as he passed the benches that faced the open deck. In the wind he put his arms out and grasped the railing, hanging his head down between his shoulders. A pleasure that was half pain flooded May as she watched him against the blue sky.

Well, that young man has cut a path into my heart. He has, Mr. Dempsey. You know how I am.

I'd say I do. That was how Dempsey would have answered, in a voice hoarse and tolerant, if he had had a voice. Where was Dempsey, was he alive? How heavy it would be if not, heavier than a dozen deaths closer to her, in recent years.

You'd have done the same, of course, Mr. Dempsey. We might have fallen for each other, if we were ourselves.

We might indeed.

You met my daughter. I met your son. My son—you know he died. Though she could not think how Mr. Dempsey would have been told about Nick.

I do. I know everything.

Frieda said, "What's he say? Sven. Where's he off to?"

"Going to jump," May said. Lately she could get out these short sentences and be understood.

"Jump! Ach, God," cried Frieda. "He can't leave us on the boat."

"Juh—kidding," May said. She got up and pulled her sweater tight, determined to go out into the water-chilled air.

It was still early in the day. Very early Renee had come calling softly down the hall to waken them in time for the ferry. Even so they had been too slow, hurrying out across the wet flagstones after an early breakfast of fake scrambled eggs, getting the straps of their tote bags hooked in their sweater sleeves, and sending Sven back into the building after the sunscreen and Frieda's insulin cartridges. Nita and Nalda were grumbling sleepily. Sven refused to make a third trip, for Nita's Walkman. He was impatient, verging on angry, and hurrying them as May had not known him to do before. Renee was no help. Still in her guard's uniform she was beckoning to Sven from the lounge doorway every time he went inside. Once she caught him by the arm but he shook her off.

"Oh, it doesn't matter all that much," Charlotte chided him. "Renee, would you bring us a quick coffee? And one for you too. It's made, in my office. I know I said the early ferry, but let's be loose. We're going to see the bees. We're going to have fun!"

"We said the eight o'clock." Sven threw the last things into the back of the van without a glance at Charlotte. "Get in," he said roughly to the last of them, the clumsy new man, Mr. Tower, and he tossed in Mr. Tower's satchel and the back cushion he took everywhere with him.

Charlotte's pink face peered into the van. She stuck her thumb up. "OK, folks, looks like we're set."

May grabbed for her.

"What, dear? Oh, Mr. Dempsey. He went to the hospital last night, I'm sorry to say. I haven't heard yet. Aren't you pretty today?" Charlotte had picked this up from Renee. She leaned in and fussed with May's hair until Sven gunned the motor.

On the freeway Mr. Tower, the clergyman, who was not detached from worldly things, or restrained in manner, or even polite, not used to things at the center yet, began to complain that he did not have his knee brace. It had been with his bag. "I'm sorry," Sven said. "I'm *sorry*." He was driving very fast, but it didn't matter because there was no traffic; they had three lanes to themselves. In the mirror he glanced at Tower hunched tight-lipped in the middle seat. "I mean it, Mr. Tower, I'm sorry. Charlotte will find it, she won't miss a thing. Don't worry."

Even so, they raced up to the ticket booth too late, the ferry had not pulled away from the dock but all the cars had boarded. "Christ!" Sven said, and in the emptied lot he got out and slammed the door.

From the direction of the ticket booth a girl in khaki pants and shirt came running down the lot. Panting and angry she shoved a paper bag into Sven's hands. Pills, the knee brace, something for the brother-in-law?—Charlotte must have sent somebody after them.

So they would have to wait, first in line for the next ferry. But no, Sven was jumping in, starting the van, letting up the clutch so fast they all lurched in their seatbelts. The ticket-taker in his neon orange harness was waving them over; there was room after all. They jolted onto the ramp and drove deep into the cavernous ferry, which was half empty.

Before they could get down from the van the ferry was under way, and before anyone could tell her not to, May went over to the chain being hooked by a boy in overalls to a pole in a socket, across the huge open car bay where the deck dropped off. She stood on the oily floor watching the water churn out behind them. Her hair blew all over her face and into her mouth.

It was that moment of elementary happiness when the land is left behind and the expectation fills you that something will happen, something has been greeted, joined, agreed to, something to free you. She felt that same bay yawn in herself, and her spirit swoop to the wide entrance and dip as if to drink.

"Come on!" From the stairway to the passenger deck the others were calling her faintly over the engines and the wind. She realized as she turned to follow them that she had been waiting weeks to smell the deep fishy cold Pacific water that ran into the Sound, and to hear gulls squawk, swiveling their heads to peer into the ferry as they banked on the offshore wind.

On the passenger deck she could feel the floor tremble with the steady grinding progress of the vessel. The ferry's shadow rode on green water that had its own purple undershadow, and morning sun on the surface in a million loose rings.

Soon the wind let up and the water relaxed into larger, sliding rings, linking and unlinking. At a certain point the near water became the far, and at that point it was milled into kernels. Glorious water and sky. The sky was filled with very white scraps of cloud. Everyone should be breathing this air, everyone should be borne slowly upward and down, sitting at a table. But Charlotte had kept the child Jean-Baptiste from his ferry ride, caused Renee to fight with Sven before the sun was up, left her in the hall with her hands clasped behind her neck and her elbows drawn together in front of her mouth, a silver track on each dark cheek.

May did not go out onto the deck, because at that moment a man moved out from under the yellow light to Sven's side and began to talk to him. The man had a young, dried-up, nervous face. He had on torn shorts and had not taken the trouble to shave, which caused May to dismiss her first idea that he was trying to pick Sven up.

The two talked at the rail while she stood undecided. She sat back down to get her breath. "It's cold out there!" Nita ventured, and she and Nalda, just now fully awake, shivered elaborately. When May tried to prop her cane it fell on the floor. "Look at you!" Frieda said while she was bent over scraping to get it out from under the chair. Frieda snatched the cane up and presented it to her. "Now *put*—the *wrist*—in the *loop!*"

When May looked again the man was not there, so she wrapped herself in the sweater, pulled her hands inside her sleeves, and set off for the foredeck. The gulls were circling and fighting, diving after French fries someone had thrown over the side. Sven whirled. "May! What are you doing out here?" When she had sleeves, hands, and cane in order enough to get a grip on the rail, he said, "So—did you want some coffee? Careful," and he took her arm. "Time for coffee."

"No." She jerked her elbow away. *"Here."* She swayed.

Before she knew it, though, he had steered her back to the table with Frieda and the giggling twins, and closed her hand around a Styrofoam cup of very black coffee. She didn't know what else to do so she took a sip and burned her tongue. "Oh Sve-yen!" cried Nita. "Where's *Renee?*"

Sven was already heading for the deck. "Back at the ranch," he called over his shoulder, unsmiling.

Losing sight of him, May pulled herself up out of the chair. She had broken into a sweat, her weak leg shook. Who did he think he was? She was not going to be hauled back and forth against her will, she was going out onto the deck. She was going to please herself. Draw in enough sun and sky to last her the dark wet months.

"There she goes again," Frieda screeched after her. "She'll fall!"

By herself May could think and look, under the open sky that had turned a deeper blue. Fewer clouds now, just white puffs here and there like ducks on a pond. And real ducks—ducks were out in the middle of the Sound with them, diving under and when it seemed too late for them to have any breath left, far from where they had gone down, coming up through the shimmying, elongating rings. May tried to get her own breath.

Ahead you could see the Olympics. Below the forested slopes there was a land of meadows, hidden from sight. And Charlotte's sister's bees would be out all day in their thousands, out and back, stirring the flowers and massing in the inland fences overgrown with blackberry. Out and back. And the idea of coming back to rest, or for good, troubled not a one. A bee's life of effort, of unforced, pitiless agreement. Yet how the bodies twitched, and whirled off, as if in a passion. She hoped they would see some of that on this trip. The message bringing and the shooting off in pursuit and the ecstatic burrowing, not just the boxed seething.

She was a rare thing, Charlotte would sing, off-key, when they came in to lunch after having their hair set. *Fine as a bee's wing.*

By herself May could think. She turned over the events of the morning. The voices in the hall, Mr. Dempsey. The freeway, the rush down the empty lanes at the terminal, the young woman who ran up to Sven. How she ran pell-mell across the asphalt, angry, with the paper bag in her hands . . .

May gasped. Her heart did something unpleasant, probed her chest rudely twice, three times, and then began to hammer.

She went as fast as she could, past Tower stretched out on a window seat, snoring with his hand on his stained vest in a vague ecclesiastical gesture. She thought of saying, "Help me. Come with me," but she went on by herself.

Sven was back at the table, refereeing while Nita and Nalda played a game piling their hands together and pulling them out. Frieda had turned her back disgustedly. May dropped the cane a second time. With difficulty, sitting down to do it, she rescued it from under the table, and when she sat up the blood had all run to her head. That was good. *"Van,"* she said to Sven, with some force. *"Van."* She stabbed her finger downward. She rolled her eyes and grasped the table.

"Uh oh," he said. "Stay up here, why don't you, if you're sick. You can lie down." He pointed at Tower asleep.

"No."

"No? Over there's the restroom."

"No. Van." She made her eyes fierce. She was making him let her. She was his favorite.

They both considered the likelihood of her falling down the stairs. She knew him. She saw him consider that it would be a choice, of a kind, if she were to fall down the stairs. She saw him decide, against his own interests as the one who would be blamed, to let her go. For no other reason than because she wanted to.

But he stood up. "I'll come with you." He rummaged in his pocket for the keys.

"No." She waved a finger admonishingly, like a teacher, with a nod of her head to indicate the twins. The twins could not be left. They could wander and disappear. At the center they wore wanderers' bracelets that beeped if they approached a door.

"Stay here!" Nalda cajoled. "Watch this!"

May set off. She went slowly, keeping her back straight and her dragging leg firm so that Sven wouldn't follow her. She managed the stairs, and used her cane all the way to the middle of the half-empty car deck before she discovered she had come out of the stairwell on the wrong side, so that she had to circle the bay to find the van at the end of the line of cars. With her good left hand she fought with the lock on the rear door.

In the well was the paper bag the girl had handed to Sven.

Who was she, in the uniform—hadn't she been wearing a uniform? A khaki uniform like Renee's. Was she a guard like Renee? But not like Renee. Renee in the doorway saying, "Dohn do that," in despair.

There were two cardboard boxes in the bag, each the size of a large book, heavily bound with duct tape. She took them out of the bag and turned them over in her hands. She didn't shake them, she didn't need to.

How would he do it? How pass the boxes to whoever was waiting for him? He would find some excuse to stop. Easy to pull into a gas station or a parking lot. None of them would get out, just Sven with his packages. There was nobody else in charge, nobody with them to see what Sven did, or protect him. Nobody would even remember he had stopped. Or if they did they wouldn't say; he was counting on their approval of him, their vain, hopeless liking.

She went around to unlock the door on the passenger side. Standing on the step she got the glove compartment open and looked among the little paper cups. Maybe there would be a nail file or a penknife so she could open the boxes.

Lying on the maps was Renee's gun.

So Sven was going alone. He was going to drop them all off at Charlotte's sister's, to see the bees. He was not going to hand the packages off on the way, he was going to make up something and while they were looking at chunks of honeycomb or drinking their Gatorade he was going to drive away in the van. He was going to meet somebody in person, on that man's territory. In one of the machine shops clustered around the shipyard, or in a guard's booth, or in one of those warehouses full of barrels and catwalks that she knew from the movies. And for this he would be paid, wasn't that right? Of course he was going to do it that way.

After a bit she got one box slit open using the car key. Exactly. Exactly. In neatly taped plastic bags, and like cornstarch, but looser.

She dug in her tote bag for her wallet. She always had cash in her wallet, she didn't let them get near it in the center to investigate. Right now she had four hundred dollars. She would give it to Sven when she told him what she had done, and furthermore tell him what she had in the bank. "It's yours," she would say. "But use it for your life." She should have done it long ago. Why hadn't she helped him? She should have told Renee. Renee could have made him take it, told him, "Have it, she want you to have it."

"What are you doing?"

By this time she wasn't doing anything, just holding on, looking over the side of the car deck at the water. The sun rings could not be seen. Here the water hissed up pale green, closer, and swarmed and doubled back in confusion, though you did not feel it in the motions of the ferry, which were broad and regular.

"Threw—over." She showed him with her hands.

Sven looked at the empty paper bag, and at her, long enough to test what she said, and then past her, his eyes making a wild sweep of the whole car deck. He shook his head. His hand ran up and down the steel upright with paint rusted into sharp edges, and then with both hands he grabbed it and leaned out as far as he could to scan the water. His face around the thin-skinned nose had turned the marble color of his fingers. He dropped from the upright and slumped against the van, and for a second May was relieved, until he said, doubling over, "God, God."

A sound issued from her, a voice. "No, 'Ven. Don't—do." No consolation, no proof she could offer that his life, all postponement and longing so far, would shake itself free.

She was going to go on, hand him the money she had in her fist, but he spread his fingers on his forehead and plucked as if there were strings there. He blew his breath out twice and said, "I'm dead. They'll kill me."

Her knees gave. Over the thrashing water her eyes focused out and out as if her sight could escape her and go on, but it had to come back to him crouched in front of her. Of course. He would arrive without the boxes and they wouldn't believe him. Of course. Of course. *They'll kill me.*

What had she done?

She pressed her fists into her ribs. He didn't move his hand from his eyes but he said, "Wait a minute. Wait."

No way to make up for it. May tottered, as she had when the boxes lay on the green water bobbing away. Sven unbent his body and she made ready for him to hoist her up in his arms and cram her over the sill into the water. Get rid of her.

"Calm down," Sven was saying. "Calm down." He was catching her as she swayed. Now his face was dead white, with dull ovals where his fingers had pressed, but he spoke with a dazed reasonableness. "All right. I see. I getcha."

What had taken the place of crying, with May? She wanted to cry but where tears would have come from she had an inner forceps working on her. She wanted to say she had gone crazy, she could not think straight, not anymore, she had made the awful mistake of thinking she could reason and act, she was sorry, she would be sorry from now on. She could make her lips move but not produce a sound. Her fingers were squeezing the folded bills while her legs, like poles in loose holders, shifted her with the sways of the ferry. The ferry was slowing down. Sven took her by the arm and shoulder. The engines thundered harder, the gulls flashed by, their open beaks making no sound over the proud mechanical roar.

"You stay here. I'm going back up, I got a friend of mine watching the others. Hey now, wait a minute. You sit. Sit." She nodded dizzily. "Don't move. Calm down." It occurred to her he thought she might die on him now. He boosted her into the van. His eyes squinted past her as she rallied her good hand and pressed the bills into his pocket. "Wrote me a note? Hey, a note about it. Jesus, calm down." Humbly she pulled herself up by the seatbelt, gasping for air. Her heart had pirated her lungs. She would sit down and let shame burn tunnels into her until she was ash.

"You stay here. I'll bring the others." His voice was tired and hard.

Righteous, awful woman, she was keening to herself. *Awful, awful woman, why were you born?* But it was not anything so righteous, what she had done.

She let herself think so, finally. It was not anything for the good of other people, poor or rich, those people she knew waited angrily, desperately, in the little city of shipyard workers and sailors, for the cocaine or heroin or whatever it was—or perhaps they merely waited in seeming indifference, like the starlings in the trees, though not, not ever, expert in their greeds and refusals as the starlings were. No, she had not done it to spare those people.

If only she had Mr. Dempsey now, to sit beside her. *Mr. Dempsey . . . Samuel . . . I have done the wrong thing.*

She had not been able to think it through. She sat for a long time and then she opened the door. She climbed down slowly and squeezed between the van and the car in front of it, catching her pants leg on the license plate. Finally she got the door on the driver's side unlocked. Throwing her cane into the back she climbed heavily into the driver's seat. There, as if a hand had been laid firmly on her to dispense with all the lurching in her mind, she came into possession of herself.

She had the sensation of *driving.* Driving her own car, as she had—could it have been only months ago?—when she was a woman with plans to visit her daughters, and time to spend at the movies and at restaurant tables with wine before her, a woman of the world—but, oh, had she not insulted the world, said inexcusable things about it? That she was tired of certain restaurants. Tired of pigeons on her balcony. Her own balcony! Pigeons! With their low thrilled note so tender compared to the spit-spit of the center's starlings—and even that note a sound she had come to listen for—slow, aggrieved pigeons, occasionally leaving a mess on the open gangway, which might have been a path down a green field for the spasm it caused her to think of it now, above the courtyard in the quadrangle where her building had been, still was. Where an old man she never met used to come out and grasp the rail of his two-foot balcony like a sea captain, and search the sky.

Tired of the way people drove.

The steering wheel in her hands surprised her. A simple thing, ring an inch thick, obeyed by a machine weighing tons. You would never suspect the satisfaction you would find in a thing like that, or that you had been longing for it. If only she could sit forever without being seen, holding the wheel and giving it sturdy turns. With both hands on it she put her head back in an envy of everyone who could drive, everyone not herself.

But that sank away. Something had approached her as she sat vacant and still. Now it entered. By its weight it seemed to be sadness, but if that was it, it was the ecstatic sadness she had last known—when? In the Depression. Twelve or thirteen, she would have been, leaning out the open bathroom window on a cold night with her hair in a towel.

Dark would have fallen, silencing the voices in the house, blotting up the echoes of the talk at dinner, of falling wages and crop failures and lynchings. The dark sky, the moon coming up would send a sad thrill along her cold arms. How tenderly she pitied the family downstairs, her parents and sister, along with anyone else not herself! *She* was going to be a scientist, not a tired well-meaning doctor in practice like her father, but the possessor of a laboratory and the means to pass out to everyone the cures she discovered. Or she would be a writer, or be singled out in some manner to hold power, to bring a halt, all over the country, to this downward rush. Even though downstairs all was as it should be, must be, her mother and father in their appointed places, her mother working on an article about the starving veterans who had set up camp in Washington, D.C., until the army marched on them.

But May would not be like her mother, with her petitions, her picket signs. If people were still brutal by then, she would be in a position to talk them out of it, and give them jobs. They wouldn't have to be thieves or hobos anymore, or drink themselves to death.

The moon was hers, she could almost squeeze it like the lemons they had given up buying, and pour it down her throat, while steam ran off her head and arms into the cold air. But that was when the peculiar sadness would strike. Unaccountably struck from her rapture, she would begin to wonder why it was she went through soaping herself all over and wrapping a towel around her so many thousands of times, when the moon was a *thing,* rising unaware of any human, alive or dead, and how many humans shivered looking on it at that very moment, with their strange bulging organs of sight? Who could they be? Who could she be? Why should they exchange oxygen and carbon dioxide and live? And she would wish to cry but find no tears, only her own blankness, her blank body in a towel—visible in the mirror if she glanced over, a pinkish solid with maps of bath powder on it. She shrank from her body. Even then it did not always obey her. It woke her up at night, it demanded sensations. She really didn't want it to be hers, to be her.

This was a sadness that called for an expelling motion, for flinging the water out of her hair, running on wet feet, throwing herself on the bed.

Her sadness now was the same, half a grave suspicion, half an odd, satiating, invited pleasure. It had an authority, a cold, like witch hazel on the skin. Where had it come from into her, making some sort of blind directive motion like a semaphore? *This way.*

Their lateness. They were late onto the ferry. They were last. The van was last in line. Behind it the open Sound, and all would be explained, and Sven come to no harm.

She had it now, as she had not when she made her way down the steps with her cane and her plan. He had left her the keys.

She was still leaning back resting, in this state in which she could know and wonder, before she sat up smartly and looked at her watch, rolled her window down and leaned over to get the passenger window. Even with the windows open the van would wonder and pause, with that machine ignorance, that sad poetry of the machine, that obedience, and pitch up—she was guess-ing—before it nosed down with the weight of the engine.

Very likely she would try, through the open window—she was strong on one side anyway, from the machine they had made her row all spring—she would try mightily to push herself up to the surface where the million rings were sparkling. She would not waste time ashamed of trying; her body would try for her. A body was possessive of itself, blood racing like this at the amorous speed she remembered from nicotine. No one could say, for an-other, what was despair and what the fiercest pleasure.

There was the clutch for the thinking foot, the gas for the heavy one. That was good. With the clutch out the left foot could push the other. Her fingers stayed awake on the key. *Ignition,* she said to herself.

A man in neon orange would come skidding across the oily deck the minute the engine turned over. But she had always been efficient, in a car. In her dream she had driven two cars at once! Her body would remember for her, answer for her, loyal current down the left arm crossed under the wheel and wobbling the gearshift. She didn't look in the mirror at the ferry's open bay to gauge the distance she had to accelerate.

Jam it into reverse.

The van lunged, with a roar she felt more than heard, the tires spun and caught. The van hit the chain flying, she felt a hideous resistance and then a skid as the chain gave at the latch and sent her sideways, and she felt the bump and shock of space to the back wheels, and the tilt into air.

She was pulled to the clean kite-spool, she was herself! She could feel her teeth and the roof of her mouth with the tongue clamped on it, and the nail beds on her fingers on the steering wheel, she could feel the hairs on her head.

SEVEN

One Life: Anna

Maybe she was not a human being. Maybe she was a silkie, like the creature that came up out of the sea and asked for the baby, in her mother's song.

"Sing your song!"

"It's not mine, it's an old, old song," her mother said.

As if she knew what May was thinking, her sister Carrie said, "The silkie's a *man*."

"It is not."

Now she was humming "Down in the Valley," so Carrie said, "That's the one *I* want." They were standing on the table in their stocking feet, having their hems pinned. The leaves of Simplicity pattern rustled as they turned. Her mother's quick, thin fingers dipped in and out, her red hair bobbed as she hummed.

" 'Hang your head over, hear the wind blow,' " May joined in, waving off flies with her toe from the plate heaped with store-bought gingersnaps.

"Quit it, May." Carrie pushed her.

May started over, louder. "'Down in the val-ley, the valley so low, hang your head ohh-ver——'" and she swayed, being turned by her mother's hands. Hot sunlight lay on the table, a long tray of it for them to stand in.

"May's bothering me again. Why does she have to sing when you sing? And she tries to stand right where I'm standing."

Just as her mother said, "I don't really think she does," everything in the room ran together in sparks, arcing and spinning— table, plate, her mother's fingers weaving pins into cloth. May almost fell. The sun had done it, making a puddle of fire on the table when she looked down.

I'm in there, she said to herself. *I'm in there where the sun is water, that's why I'm hot, I'm down in it, tiny and made of gold, or fish-silver, swimming. I don't have to go to school ever again.*

"Your daughter Carrie was clever," the teacher said. Mrs. *Pitt.* She said it after school to May's mother, who was only passing the time of day, not looking for a narrow-minded analysis of her daughters, either one, as she told their father at dinner. "I enjoyed having Carrie," Mrs. Pitt went on. "But May . . . Now May, I was saying to Mrs. Olafsson in the second, May Harkness has a bit too much respect for herself. The child——" But there Mrs. Pitt had stopped, or there May's mother with her dark eyebrows drawn together had stopped her.

There was no word anyway for what May was. *I am from far away. I am from Sule Skerrie.*

May knew she was as smart as Carrie but something kept Mrs. Pitt from knowing it. It might have been her failure to learn to read all year. She knew the letters but they were so many seeds scattered on the page, and would not grow words. What did it matter? She cared only for Flying Dutchman at recess and for sharing a desk with the smiling wordless Isabel, whose dark curls brushed the paper along with her St. Christopher medal as they were printing the letters of the alphabet—or as Isabel was. Isabel's rough, glossy hair gave off powerful waves of something that entered May's nostrils the way the twisting ribbon of scent from the pieman's basket entered Simple Simon's, in the book. The picture book. May couldn't see why anyone would give up a picture book, ever, for reading-books with no pictures, as Mrs. Pitt said they all would.

"Nonsense," her mother said. "Is that any way to inspire you? Just say you'll decide for yourself."

"But politely," her father spoke up, "in case Mrs. Pitt hasn't read her Kropotkin."

"You'll decide for yourself, *thank you,*" said her mother.

Isabel was a shy girl with a faraway smile, who took shape maddeningly in May's mind at all times of the day and night, silently winding black hair onto her white finger. The hair, with its flowery smell, was washed more than May's and Carrie's was. Isabel's mother said so. In their own bathroom with its shared towels and mangled soap, May did not think to ask to have her hair washed more often or to wash it herself, but she basked in the mild yet important scent emanating from Isabel's. It lent Isabel holiness, in the form of a sweet, indefinably pitiful aura.

With her pale pink timid lips turned up at the corners and her perfect letters rounded like beads of sago, Isabel would have been a namby-pamby but for the black-haired, extenuating beauty. "Isabel Barr was my introduction," May would tell her own daughters, "despite having a mother and a sister, to femininity."

"Whatever that is," her daughter Vera would say.

In May's house three of them were females, but by accident, it seemed. Nothing graceful or instinctive entered into their getting dressed in the morning or putting things away in their drawers, or governed their bodies and faces and voices. Everything just came out any old way. May knew that, after she had been to Isabel's house and seen the order of the bedrooms, the dressers, the linen closet, and then had questions put to her by Isabel's mother, who had on a cream-colored middy blouse and a skirt that ended above her knees, and had buffed her fingernails until they glowed like the opal in May's favorite ring. In one afternoon Isabel's mother taught them how to dance the Charleston and how to squeeze furled borders of icing from a pastry bag.

When May's mother danced she didn't do the neat-footed Charleston but ripped off her glasses and whirled into a rampage through the downstairs, if Carrie began on "The Skaters" or "The High School Cadets" at the piano, and she would grab May in her arms and whirl her too, until they flopped together over the back of the couch.

If her mother had good clothes they were given away or forgotten in the closet; she had worn her black watch plaid coat for so long May could remember no other. Only later did it come to May that she might have had a style, with her wound scarves, her big felt hat or her old, shiny little pre-war hat of black circled feathers, her georgette dresses under faded sweaters sagging with cable. She sewed; she could make each daughter a dress in a weekend, but she didn't go picking over trays for buttons of painted enamel the way Isabel's mother did, and she didn't smock their dresses or drop the waists or do anything but gathers for a skirt. By Sunday night she would be back at her desk typing out articles, her own and other people's, for the *Union-Record*.

She was writing about thugs who beat men rightfully on

strike and left them half dead on their own doorsteps, and about women no different from herself except that they were the sole support of children, and they fainted from hunger at their sewing machines. "Why don't we take them *food!*" Carrie offered in her prissy school voice.

"No, no," their mother said, "charity is not the answer. Don't you see, it's wrong, wrong, wrong, *wrong.*"

May prided herself on understanding this as Carrie did not. She knew it by heart: mutual aid was a law of nature, charity a trick. It was Kropotkin.

When their father came in late from the clinic he liked to be read aloud to in front of the fire while he ate his dinner with a big wooden tray across his lap. Carrie lay wrapped in a blanket on the rug, blocking the fire's heat, and didn't listen; she was noisily turning her own pages, calling attention to the special assignments she got every day because she was ahead.

Propped against the marble clock was a photograph of their mother with a group of women posed outdoors in winter coats, in two rows of chairs, arm in arm with their hat brims touching. Around their necks hung beautifully lettered signs saying NO WAR. Her mother had marched against conscription at the side of a woman named Anna Louise Strong.

"But your mother," their father said, "was slightly in the lead."

No War. It seemed to May in the first grade that she could read those words, if no others.

"May smells! Does she have to go down there with the chickens and then come in my room?" Every day Carrie complained, even though the bedroom belonged to both of them for the time being, while May was little and needed company.

After school May was in the habit of ducking into the chicken house she and Carrie had used as a hideout before summer ended and the days took the cramped shape of first grade. Now that it was almost summer again May went by herself, tired as she often was after school, and irritated, with skinned knees and all the voices of the day in her head. She didn't even mind the spiders Carrie hated, hanging in corner webs and living, their father said, on a diet of bird lice.

The chickens belonged to him. They had arrived in two squawking crates for his birthday. Chickens were no longer kept in their neighborhood, though an old fenced chicken house stood in a corner of the yard, half covered with blackberry vines. Their father worried but their mother said, "No one will mind. They're no different from the MacLeods' beehive." Now in the morning when May was lugging the bucket of laying mash, Mr. MacLeod waved his big glove cheerfully at her. He let her come over and watch from a safe distance as the bees shot in and out of the hive.

Once quite by chance she and her father had seen the whole hive emerge. They had been burning a leaf with a magnifying glass, when suddenly next door the bees poured upward in a giant brown question mark and hung on a branch in their own yard, like a big sweater thrown into the tree. "It's just the old queen gone up in yer spruis tree," Mr. MacLeod called. "She's wanting to leave us, but I shan't let her."

The chickens came to her father at their foolish armless trot and bumped his ankles like cats, and he petted them as if they were cats. Her mother had been right to give him chickens. At one time, he told May, long ago in the colonies, people had thought nothing of dropping a hen down a chimney to clean it. "Clean a chicken?"—but it was the chimney. He told her stories of the turkeys his own father had raised in the Skagit Valley, so big they could knock a man over. Then, sent to medical school by his prosperous grandmother, the one in the long black dress on the study wall, he met a college girl.

Oh, all he was doing was going down a hill in Boston, and she coming up, a redhead. An Irish girl, a beauty. Their mother! You could almost see in those eyes, he said, the political wrangling in the hot whiskey-smelling kitchen where he would soon be pulling up his chair with all the suspicious Irish brothers.

The girl who was to be May's mother handed him a leaflet that said KEEP OUT. Out of the war, it meant, the Great War. May liked to hear the story, the pieces fitting one by one: the turkeys, the black dress, the hill, KEEP OUT.

May got in the habit of sitting in the chicken house. When she liked a thing she liked it painfully and had to do it or have it or see it over and over. Her mother understood and somehow approved, but it was one of the things Carrie hated about her. Carrie hated all the old pleasures now, and liked only rows of multiplication and division, and clapping the chalk out of blackboard erasers after school for the teacher, and whispering under the horse chestnut trees with the girls in fourth grade all through recess, instead of playing Flying Dutchman or joining the relays in preparation for Field Day or even pitching chestnuts at the boys for them to stamp on and squash.

The only time Carrie was her old self was when she got out of bed in the middle of the night. To her shame she was a sleepwalker. May could follow and take hold of her if she did it gently, but Carrie would drag back with a foolish face, at first shy and then cross, as you might show a waterlogged resentment if you blundered into Green Lake with your clothes on the way a very old woman had done before their eyes, so that their father had to wade in after her and bring her back, and calm her family running down the hill from their picnic.

When she was sleepwalking Carrie was herself, she was back to being May's sister, as stubborn and alone as May felt herself to be. From the front hall where she could usually be found on the bench of the hat rack, or steering along the inlaid stripe of walnut on the floor, Carrie let herself be led upstairs. She never really woke up at all, while May would lie for an hour afterward, cold and listening. As the light came in May could hear a high continuing tone in the room, like a hissing chime. She liked to be the only one awake. She liked to hear the first notes, single as passwords, of the starlings her father said were invading the city.

Their mother went to bed very late, or she went to bed and then got up again to read and proofread and clean the house— though they could not really see what had been cleaned, or why she would not have someone come in to do it. Carrie dusted, by choice, after her discovery of a mold growing between the piano keys. Sometimes in the study May found an old cup of her mother's strong sugared tea with a different mold, a disc of waving softness, asleep in it. She liked to look into this tea, and slosh the tentative blue-green thing. If Carrie found it she would splash it into the sink and scour the cup, and call for May to get the mold with her fingers and throw it into the garbage pail.

At any rate their mother would have just gone to sleep in the dark of early morning, which was when Carrie's sleepwalking took place. Their father too slept heavily, though he could be wakened by the telephone. Often he was gone half the night delivering a baby and no one even knew it. "Thank heavens we can rely on May to get you back in bed," he told Carrie.

Carrie said, "She does not."

At school May got into trouble for tripping the boys and for luring Isabel into the mudhole at the bottom of the playground, where everything Isabel had on, down to her tiny silver watch— not even Isabel could tell time!—was stained and clogged and spoiled when she fell, just *let* herself fall.

May had to stand in the corner for disturbing others and shouting and lagging, and for talking back. For a "spirit of dispute." Things she would have paid for if she had been a boy. The boys were spanked, and occasionally paddled with a bread paddle sent up from the basement kitchen for the purpose.

At school Carrie pretended they were not sisters, and liked her no more. Her mother said that was not so, though it might seem so. Sometimes May could hold her breath and make a pressure of hate in her own head, but she couldn't keep it there. Her eardrums gave once, twice, like bike brakes, and the air burst out of her.

In the watery light slanting into the chicken house she heard her mother's voice say through the vents, "A sad girl came this way. You chicks, give her some eggs."

"'A mischief that is past and gone,'" was what her mother would say when one of them complained of something the other had done, unless there was a lie involved. When that happened she would take off her glasses and lay her cigarette in its groove in the pewter ashtray. "I don't understand. If *both* of you are telling the truth . . ." Without her glasses, they knew, she couldn't see much more than their shapes. It was her heavy sad eyebrows drawn together that stopped them. Though Carrie never gave in to shame, and would always stand by a lie. Nothing in their mother's face, pale under its freckles, was felt as a reproach by Carrie later, or made her brood on what she had done, or even remember it. She was not troubled, as May was, by anything hotly sorrowful, anything locked away and private in her feelings for their mother, anything uneasy.

Their mother had no religion, even though she had been raised a Catholic as their father said an Irish girl must be. But she had superstitions. She believed for instance that some spirit had hovered at the naming of her daughters. May was May Olivereau, named for an anarchist; Carrie was Caroline Verona, named for the ship that had carried the union martyrs shot in Everett the year before her birth. "Both of you have *v-e-r* in your names, through no intention of ours," their mother said. "You see? *V-e-r* is the root of *truth.*"

Coming out of the schoolhouse May went still with dread every day before she identified her mother, so slight among the women waiting in a group that she could have been a seventh grader let out before the bell. When May caught sight of her in her plaid coat her ribs hurt, she shut her eyes, she bolted forward until she came to a stop against her mother.

This shock at the end of each hated day of the first grade— the scalding relief of seeing her mother's glasses flash, and locking her fingers onto the big tortoiseshell buckle of her mother's coat—May outgrew, to her surprise. When she crossed the hall from Mrs. Pitt to Mrs. Olafsson for second grade she waited for it and it wasn't there; it lost itself until many years later, when as a married woman she came upon the same dread, relief, and joy with a man not her husband.

In the second grade—the year of the soothing and boring Mrs. Olafsson, whose big slow-moving hips and pinned-up braids and soft monotonous voice daily lulled May into a semi-sleep at her desk—she swore off Carrie. She did it the way her mother was always swearing off cigarettes. She swore off the past of playing with Carrie and talking to her in bed at night, though Carrie might relent when the light was off, and toss in her bed sighing things to herself so May would have to say, "What? What?" as if no look of stone had passed between them on the playground.

If Carrie wanted to talk and May didn't answer, Carrie flounced up onto her elbow on the pillow and hummed one of their mother's bedtime songs in a high, challenging tone:

Si bébé pas fait dodo
Gros chat est là que manger li

which had a sweet repeating tune, but meant a huge cat would eat May if she didn't go to sleep. Yet in Haiti, it was a lullaby. Their mother was full of these lullabies from other countries, and sad songs no one else knew.

"The happiest moment of your mother's life," their father said, "was when she heard Paul Robeson sing 'My Curly Headed Baby.'" He would say this fluffing the ends of Carrie's thick braids.

"And then he sang 'My Straight-Haired Baby with the Straight Eyebrows,'" their mother would be sure to say.

"He did not!" Carrie would yell, but May felt a shiver of advantage, seeing in the mirror the forceful eyebrows placed on her like her mother's own initial.

Neither of them had hair the scorched dark red of their mother's; they were both fair like their father. Their mother liked to braid their hair but she had shingled her own. "Who is this?" their father had cried out, stricken, when she did it. "Is this the new paperboy?" But in a day or two he was admiring the hair, cupping its straight edges in his hands and kissing their mother in the white-skinned parting.

He put a feed bin in the chicken house for May to sit on. Two of the chickens, he had agreed, were hers to pull in her wagon if she could get them to sit in it. She no longer did that; she could not say just what it was she liked now about the chickens, and required of them.

They were Plymouth Rocks, with the white bars woven into the dark feathers like hem tape, no two exactly alike. At first she did not speak to them in their boxes, but sat watching their sequin eyes blink up from below in the way they had if you looked at them for any length of time, as if your rudeness were no more than they expected, as they drifted into the tucked sleep of birds, who would never deign to squirm or wheeze or sprawl helplessly in their beds with drool on the pillow and a leg hanging, the way May often found herself when she woke up. When she did speak they cocked their heads the merest bit, acknowledging the events she related, and belittling them. They had no sympathy. Her voice—"I can't read! I'm the only one!"—seemed to soothe them. *Alphabet!* The bright eye winked. *Sister! What of it?* The chickens would blink and settle, blink and ruffle and settle, as if she were putting them to bed with a story, the implausible story of what happened in human life, and hearing it they would only occasionally snap awake, whip their heads to one side as if she had shown them one of themselves skinned for the dinner table, and gape for a long time, their thin tongues poised in the air.

May never wanted to hear about narrow escapes, or miracles of recovery. Even before her mother got pneumonia she didn't like the healings in the Bible stories their father read them. Why one blind man and not all the others?

What religion there was in the house was their father's responsibility. Their mother's view was that religion was usually to be found locked in the arms of drink. "I should know the comfort it is, from a-many Irish funerals," she liked to say, rolling her eyes.

Because he was a doctor their father said, "You don't see them when they require the comfort of religion," but then he had to take it back, of course. They all knew the story of the influenza epidemic. It was before their father moved his new family out of Boston. With a baby of her own to take care of, their mother had nursed both her parents until, three days apart, they died. May and Carrie would never see Boston; their mother would never go back, never.

They heard about these things, scraps of them, at the dinner table. The padlocked schools, the empty sidewalks. The word out not to gather for funerals. *Epidemic.* Their mother almost falling out a third-floor window as she shouted at a milk wagon, which clopped on around the corner. Their grandmother's whispered wish, on her last day, for a tea their mother could not buy for her because the flu had closed the stores.

All the while in her draped bassinet, in furious rosy health, the new baby kicked and screamed. That was Carrie. Her baby screams filled Boston. Boston took its shape for May from the word *boss,* from her mother's talk of mill workers and longshoremen. *Boston*: shouts, cruel orders, indifference, death. And she could see the little stupidly waving fists of her sister, who didn't know to be quiet in the bassinet while her grandmother was dying. I *would have been quiet,* May thought. I *would have known.*

And of course their mother's life had always been finding out, and putting down on paper for others to know, whatever happened that was unjust, cruel, and terrible. May knew that.

Sometimes after dinner their mother would read aloud from an article she was writing, or from a book she was reading herself. Her hero was Kropotkin. Despite her boredom, May listened to the part about animals helping each other. "Charity . . . is a trick," her mother would read, with a proud smile at May, just as she would pause and give May a special look in the suspense that followed "The king . . . sent . . . for his messenger." *Kropotkin,* May said to herself, feeling a vague satisfaction. Like catkin, or Nutkin from her book. She was seven. She formed a picture of the man with this name: a small man, black button eyes, a boy, really. As her mother's hero, Kropotkin would have a burning wish, and it would not be anything her sister Carrie would wish for, but her mother's wish and her own, for *happiness.* But happiness *for everyone.* The strange, thrilling, mournful longing that belonged to her mother and now to her, that no one suffer. A bodily feeling both restless and sleepy in May as she listened—as sickish as hanging in midair in a dream trying to stay up once you had jumped off a cliff and were flying.

Once her mother read them a story from a magazine, the *Atlantic Monthly.* It was a very old issue, more than twenty-five years old, she said, smoothing the wrinkled pages, and it had no cover. "The sweet Kropotkin," she said before she began, smiling at May alone.

But this thing was so awful May could not believe anyone sweet had written it down. It was about torture. May still could barely read, although Mrs. Olafsson was finding ways to teach her. *Torture* she felt as a torch. But it was really a punishment inflicted on boys hardly any older than Carrie, who was ten—at this Carrie shuddered dramatically under the afghan by the fire and covered her ears—peasant boys who were expelled from their houses so the younger children could have food. The door was shut. What were they to do, these boys Carrie's age? They set off alone to *join the army*. Of course, once in the army—they were boys, after all—they broke some small rule. Then—could this be? could it be? but it must have been so long ago . . . but it wasn't, her mother said—they were dragged, dripping blood, past *a thousand men* in two lines, each man bringing down his stick on the back, the legs of the boy, while a *doctor* stood by— here their mother cast a despairing look at their father—to lift the wrist and stop the drumming sticks just before the boy's pulse came to a stop. No one dared to hold back, lest he be pulled out of the ranks and sent down the line himself.

May sat frozen on the ottoman.

"That's why she can't read, Anna." It was her father's voice on the landing, hours later. "She's afraid to read. She hears these things, they come from you. She'll never forget a thing like that."

Under the covers May slid down her bed to the footboard. *A thousand men. And the boy from Carrie's class with the bubble hanging out of his nose—they were spanking him in the hall, two teachers. Two.*

A thousand men.

She'll never forget a thing like that.

For a while after that their mother was in mild disgrace.

Though she still sang to them at bedtime, their father took over in the evenings with the Bible. It was time for that: a sensible Protestantism must be called in. They were getting older. Whatever their mother thought about it, they must carry out of childhood with them the knowledge of Joseph being handed up onto the camels of the Midianites, and Moses in the bulrushes, and Ruth in the fields of corn.

In the ninth grade, May decided that Carrie could do as she liked, but she herself would go to college and major in one of the sciences. Probably chemistry.

Her chemistry lab partner, Eugene, had a popular sister. Carrie was in the senior class with her, the beautiful Olga. Everyone knew who Olga was. She was not pretty enough to be on the homecoming court; her beauty was that of an adult woman, May thought, and so was her melancholy stare. Sometimes at school she went days barely speaking. Her tall brother coming along behind her was the same. May began, while Eugene was pouring from beakers, to notice the veins standing up in his forearms. When he rolled up his starched white shirtsleeve, the muscle rounded and clenched. What skin could be seen was oddly smooth, smoother and paler than her own.

May knew his father owned a lumberyard; later she found out from Carrie that Eugene had worked there after school since the third grade. "Third grade!" her mother said. "When will we have a law?"

Her father grinned. "Now you respect the law?"

"Some laws we need, for now."

Eugene wanted to be a scientist. May was going to be a scientist herself, although that conflicted with her wish to be a writer, but in the period before she was famous in either field she might teach school, and if so she would teach chemistry.

Eugene had inexpressive eyes the clear brown of tortoiseshell, pulled tight at the corners because his mother was Russian, said Carrie. He almost never smiled. In the cafeteria May saw Olga bow her head with its stark middle part and chew each mournful bite, surrounded by senior boys.

Eugene had chosen May. They had to do the experiments in pairs, and the teacher had the boys choose. He would have offered the privilege to the girls, he was known for saying every year, if they could have managed it without a lot of silliness beforehand. The other boys were picking boys, until boys ran out and they groaned and began on the girls. There were many more girls; boys had begun dropping out of school to look for work. But Eugene, while there were still boys remaining, said, "May Harkness."

Gradually, Carrie was becoming kindly toward May, full of advice. "Smile at him. Smile whenever he looks at you."

"I can't just smile all through chemistry."

Carrie was going to graduate, but she didn't want to go to the academy of stenography or to nursing school, or drown herself in some charity; she would not have wanted to go to college even if there had been money for it. She wanted to play the piano, go to the pictures, and take the streetcar to Green Lake with her friends. She wanted to forget Hoover and Roosevelt and the economy and the poor, and begin a life of her own choosing.

Boys sat on the glider surreptitiously playing with her curls, and laughed at anything she thought up to say, and even danced with her to records that weren't for dancing, though she giggled instead of objecting when they pulled her up to waltz to "Downhearted Blues" or "Joe Hill" or "Years are coming, speed them onward, when the sword shall gather rust," as May sat on the porch railing sourly watching.

If Eugene said, "May, where's the copper sulfate?" she felt a singing in her arms. She heard only her name. On the slate counter she traced the foreign shape of his eye with her finger. She was facing him and the big windows behind him, and if she looked long enough at the level where the dark counter stopped and the light began, a blur like a heat mirage would rise steadily for a certain distance with his silhouette in it, shimmering. The sight would give her the strange, not unpleasant sense of them all as bodies, skins filled with moving blood and chemicals and organs as unknown as the bog man just discovered in Europe. With heads on top, thinking. Batteries, her father said; the brain was a battery. But the skin, containing and shielding all this, and at the same time feeling. Did Eugene see that? Did he look at her skin?

When he told her his own name was really Yevgeny, and wrote it out with his fountain pen in the alphabet that was his as the brown eyes with their slant were his, she closed the paper in her chemistry book, drew a breath, and asked him about Kropotkin. He had never heard of Kropotkin. This made her wonder about her mother: was she right that this was a great Russian hero?

Eugene's father sat at a window looking down on a hundred workers, but his business was failing like all the others. Lately, it was said, a bottle of vodka kept him company; lately Eugene came to school with a sleepy frown, and sat with his hand over his eyes.

May tried to get her mother alone so that she could bring up the subject of Eugene, steering her away from the matter of child labor. She wanted to mention his disturbing, hypnotizing face, his smooth skin—was this skin Russian? for his sister's had the same transparency. Her mother knew all about Russians. She wanted to let her mother, in her eager way once you had her attention, begin to question her. She rarely let her mother do that now. She was ready to answer any question. She wouldn't say Eugene didn't know who Kropotkin was.

They had come downtown on the streetcar and picked their way out onto the rocks of the bay, she and her mother and Carrie. Her hair was strung across her face; she could taste the strands of it, wet and salty. She ran both hands in under her scarf and held her neck and her cold jaw. Her mother had turned her red cheeks to the wind off the water.

May was going to say something now, even though Carrie was right there two feet lower down on a rock with her magazine, sulking because she didn't want to picnic on the rocks on this cold fall afternoon with their mother, who had thrown down the article she was writing and jumped up calling, "Carrie! May! It's not raining! Let's go down to the waterfront!" Carrie wanted to go to the pictures, as they usually did on Saturday. She didn't follow the plots as May did, she sank down in the dark to wait for the man to bend the girl back for the kiss. The kiss. And it wasn't a girl half the time but a pale, married-looking woman with black lips and awful drooping eyelids. Yet May too sat transfixed every time, long after the scene was over, in a rush of sweet fright because after the kissing, she knew, came the unseen undressing, when a man crushed a woman against him and their skins touched. This she had imagined in detail.

The wind had the whole bay churning with little waves.

Where she was sitting the spray made her socks cling and mottled the skin of her knees, which she rubbed to make the ugly pattern of veins go away. "Skin's so different, on different people," she finally began, casually. "But . . ." She hesitated. That might start her mother off on the subject of race prejudice.

But her mother was gazing blankly at the water, her eyes full of tears.

May stared at her. She found she could not say, as she once would have, "What's the matter?" Why must her own heart freeze like this when her mother's face had that look?

"I'm sorry," her mother said, wiping her eyes. "Oh, I'm only thinking, thinking of my mother." She smiled apologetically.

May clenched her gloves. The water slapped the rock; she shut her lips. The epidemic. Suffering. Death. She was tired of these things. Why wasn't Carrie ever the one to ask their mother about the past, to sympathize? Her eye followed the bands of cloud upward. Water, cloud, mountain, cloud, sky. As she pretended to study the view a sort of curfew passed over it and the two long layers of cloud began to disperse. Out of the higher one came a watery disc, tinged with orange, the daytime moon.

The moon. There it was, blurred, almost humble, making its still, shy survey of the earth. " 'Come up, thou red thing,' " her mother recited slowly. " 'Come up, and be called a moon.' "

May threw her head back. She had to speak. But her mother slowly raised her arm in the plaid sleeve and held it out, whispering, "Look, girls." Hardly any distance from them a young harbor seal, its speckled hide glowing with water, was clambering onto the rock.

The seal sniffed in all directions, like a dog, before it saw them. Then for several minutes it balanced and looked, an expression of such pensiveness, such concentration in its dark eyes and black flared nose that May thought she would have to speak to it, call it, make it hers. Then it blinked, it seemed to listen, and sliding over onto its side, tail first like ribbon being turned, it sank into the water and was quickly gone.

I got a mother done gone on
Makes me feel like my time ain't long

Could this have been sung at her mother's funeral?

No. No, her father wouldn't have had that. But May had heard it. It must have been one of her mother's records. It must have been in the weeks when Carrie was submitting herself all day to records and picture albums and scraps of paper with their mother's handwriting on them. The aftermath.

It was mysterious to May that Carrie had this sickly grief in her that could not be wept out, that it was Carrie who was called to a fury of mourning that left her pretty script meandering and splotched on the black-bordered notes they were writing, and clogged her sinuses. It was mysterious, considering that May's tears came sparsely and secretly at night—as mysterious as Carrie's ability, after no more lessons than May had had, to play the piano, when she didn't care about music as May did.

Their father could not understand what had happened. For him, May thought, it had somehow not yet happened. In the middle of the night she would find herself foolishly terrified that he would *find out.*

More than once in her adult life when she was told, "So-and-so had pneumonia, but she just kept on," May heard a voice inside her rasp, *Why didn't she die?* She did not like to hear about the pneumonias people carried around with them like troublesome cats. "Oh, she fought it off. Of course she did." Women, mostly, hardy women, with their high-dose-this and their long-term-that, and their refusal to merely die. As if a person could ever have *cooperated,* in one weekend of rushed shocked dying, sitting up in bed among the newspapers while a tide from nowhere washed into her lungs.

"Bring me—" This would be a whisper; their mother would raise a burning finger and point straight up, meaning they must bring a book from the top shelf in the study. "Quick! Bring me— Gorky. *My Childhood.* And bring—oh, just that one. My Gorky in the blue wrapper." But when they came back she would not be able to hold the book, or she would have gone to sleep.

Or May read to her and she slept, breathing open-mouthed in runny strands of sound with no rhythm. " *'Look how beautiful it is!' Grandmother would exclaim, as she went from one side of the boat to the other. . . . 'Why are you crying?' 'Because I'm so happy, dear, and so old!' . . . After a pinch of snuff she would begin her wonderful stories about good robbers, saints, and all kinds of wild animals and evil spirits."*

Her father's lips had turned the gray of cement under his mustache. *"Anna,"* he kept whispering. He had the chair forward on one leg and its trembling under his weight made the floorboards quake. In the morning the fever was less but her cheeks had fallen in like thin pie dough. Now the mentholatum he had rubbed on her chest and put to melt in a saucer under the lamp covered the infected smell that came out of her open mouth. His partner, Dr. Thorp, came up the stairs and took a turn tapping and listening. *"Rales,"* he said to her father. May did not ask what that meant. She didn't look up from the page to ask about anything. She sat with her dead legs curled under her, reading on and on.

For two whole days while her mother's eyeballs twitched back and forth under the oily lids, May read the awful childhood of Gorky. Again and again, in her memory of this time, the blindly good, snuff-dipping grandmother would receive her savage beatings—she who had made the wounded starling a wing, and taught it to speak! As vividly as if they had been her own, May recalled, all her life, Gorky's fingers picking out the hairpins embedded in the old woman's scalp.

They meant nothing by it, May knew, people with their stories of walking pneumonia.

Sometimes it seemed to her that those stories, with their *almosts*—indeed all stories that ended well, and in fact the present in which people heard them with satisfaction—were a movie, full of optimism but somehow pitiless. It was another kind of story altogether that was real, from long ago, and the long ago itself where the truth of the drowning death in bed was known to everyone.

Idiots! You idiots! But she got over it. So many of her friends were younger than she. They didn't know; for them it was easy, forgivable, to say, "But wait a minute, when did antibiotics come in?"

There! in her father's *Pathology:* the lung, outside and in. Like the limp raw breast of a chicken when you peeled it off the bone. May put one hand down firmly on the book and began to tear out pages one by one, neatly, going on some way past Pneumonia before she was finished, and she threw the pages down—she, who was so superstitious about a book she didn't write her name in a new one at school when she was told to. Her father came upon the scraps on the floor. She heard his slippers stop. He picked them up without a word and closed them back into the chapter on the lung.

The decision was that May would cook, and Carrie, the neat one, would clean. But a week after the funeral it was Carrie who put on an apron and baked a sheet cake, flat and dark as the doormat, for May on her fourteenth birthday, and stuck the candles in it. At the table May unwrapped *Testament of Youth,* which she had heard her mother ordering on the telephone, and an envelope from Carrie containing a puff of cotton.

"Open it," Carrie commanded.

"I will," May said. "I will, I promise. After the cake." She knew what was in the cotton. She knew Carrie had bought her the locket they had seen in the mercantile, hanging on a velvet card. She knew what was in the locket. In the wastebasket of their mother's study she had found the photograph, where Carrie had thrown it after she cut into it with the scissors. The women in rows, and a hole above the NO WAR sign where Carrie had cut out their mother's face to fit the locket.

After she had blown out the candles their father began to mumble with his mouth full of cake, something he would never have done previously. "I remember when each of you entered this world!" He pitched forward, dropped his head into his big clean hands and cried like the worst boys spanked in school.

May locked herself in the study and pried open the pewter humidor. It was her birthday. She took a cigarette in finger and thumb and lit it, dragged deeply, rested it in the groove of her mother's ashtray. She didn't even cough.

In the days that followed she smoked the cigarettes in her mother's desk and she drank the sherry her mother kept on the sideboard. A decanter had stood there all during Prohibition for the people her mother brought back with her from picket lines, soaked to the skin. If her father smelled sherry or smoke, or if he noticed Carrie in the house in her dressing gown on schooldays, he said nothing. It took him weeks to remember his daughters at all, though when they called him he appeared, stroking his mustache and jaw in a new way that set May's nerves on edge.

His patients were calling on the telephone.

"No, of course, dear, no, we didn't really think he would be, not quite yet."

"Thank you, yes, of course we could come to Dr. Thorp. But I expect we'll wait for your father."

Carrie kept a list of the calls, crossing off the ones who knew them well enough to visit and see how things were in the house. How the house with them in it lay in the yard as if on its side.

In the rooms was an almost invisible revolving, like dust in the air or the slow heaving of their neighbor's bees, massed outside the hive on a branch of the spruce tree. Cold, Mr. MacLeod had said the bees were, cold and waiting for some order they would hear from within, to show the way. But May and Carrie heard no order. Slow fall of the nightgown, and not many hours later, slow climb back to the bedroom: why were clothes changed in this way? One piece of clothing in the morning and another at night, why were they doing it? Christmas came but they had made no preparation. The rhythm had gone out of what they did and at the same time it had gone out of what anybody did, all over the country.

Something was happening in the country to match their slowness. Things were running down. People milled around. No shouts in the lumberyards, no saws whining. Wherever a sign went up about a job, men stood in lines that doubled on themselves like material turned off the bolt into heaps on the floor.

A woman came to pay May's father with an azalea she had dug out of her yard. It was spring again. Another paid by sewing a costume for Carrie to wear in the school play. A man their father treated for arthritis worked all day on the car engine. Through the window in the gloved silence of the dining room May could see his hand with its big oily knuckles holding up the hood.

There were two things May could not forgive her father, even when in later life she became, as Carrie said, a more tolerant person. One was that as he began to lose his memory in his old age, he did not, as many did, retain the far past. He forgot her mother.

He forgot the whole segment of time from 1917 when he wed Anna, his pacifist sweetheart, as he was fond of calling her while he still remembered, through nearly two decades of the century. From 1917, the year the labor organizer Frank Little was lynched, as he himself had taught Carrie and May, the year the president went with bowed head to ask Congress for a declaration of war, to the depths of the Depression: the time that had held her.

It was not only that he had been married to their mother for nearly seventeen years and to his second wife for forty. And this was the second thing. In the company of his new wife he changed utterly. In less than a year he doted on her every bit as much as he had doted on their fierce, singing mother, though the second Anna—

Anna! a woman of the same name! a widow who had taught in their own grade school, whose husband had been his patient—had nothing remarkable of face or body or mind about her at all.

He lost his interest in politics, in justice, in society altogether; he barely read the newspaper. He lost interest in music, as Anna Olafsson did not play or care to listen. When Carrie got married to the minister at nineteen, they sent the piano to the newlyweds, strapped onto a patient's truck.

He drove Anna Olafsson to school because she didn't drive and she didn't like the streetcar, and after dinner their talk was not of the New Deal or the evil millionaires of the Liberty League, but cozy intermittent murmurings about her pupils and his patients, like the talk of old people, though she was in her early forties and he, with his gray mustache, was thirty-nine!

For Anna Olafsson he spread a load of manure with a rake, so that she could lay out her garden, and he got down on his hands and knees with her to put in tulip bulbs. She had baskets of bulbs, brought from her own closed-up house and stored in the cellar with her potatoes. May hated the tulip bulbs, piles of shut fists covered with dried dirt. They yielded creamy flowers that mobbed the yard in Anna's favorite colors, white and lavender, and had to be taken next door to the MacLeods by the armful. In April, vases and jars overflowed with them; there were always a dozen in a bowl on the dining room table, flopped open like bluish mouths.

That was part of it, for May, the colors. When her mother was alive, fiery things had lived in the house—chili peppers strung in the cellar, bought because they were beautiful hanging in the farmers' market and then forgotten, and little misshapen pumpkins with candle stumps in them, and the marigolds and rank yellow-red zinnias she brought home from meetings. And certain haunting pale orange things were hers: the fall moon in the living room window, the heavily blooming azaleas on either side of the porch steps, the yards of unmade-up satin from her trousseau, leached of their coral at the folds, in which May and Carrie had swathed themselves when they were little girls. Now suddenly there was a blue, even a lilac presence in the house, the kind of off-blue in a flowered print that had made her mother cry, "I can't sew that, that cadaver blue! That would make me sick at the machine!" A blue, double-chinned, pondering, talcum-scented presence, in the house where the first Anna had typed and sung and whirled in the living room.

May promised: *Never, never, never will I get married. They would just as soon have anybody. They don't care. They just want . . . what?*

Off her father went with the second Anna to church every Sunday. Carrie went with them. Once or twice they got May to go. It was with the sweet-faced young Methodist minister, who laid the Bible to his heart in the pulpit, and sat down frequently to the second Anna's bubbling pies, that her father and Carrie had replaced Kropotkin.

The minister's first name was Laban. Before May had ever called him by it, a tiny ruby from his mother's jewelry box was winking up and down the piano keys on Carrie's finger.

Once she was out of her teens May found she could make room for her stepmother's sturdy opinions. And later, when she and Cole had been married a dozen years or so, she began to seek them out, with their plodding, canceling assurance, their insistence that a marriage, no matter how hard-ridden, if given its head would plod to the warm stall, eat its fill, and live to run another day. Without the least sentiment about the time in her life when their droppings had been raked off the street by the ton, Anna liked the example of horses, of working or herded animals in general, and of plants, the bulbs and tubers in particular, for the hardiness missing in the newer breed of people. She offered the comfort of fish as she filleted them for flouring or poaching—fish and their cold labors. She talked of the labor of the wintered-over bulb of the tall white amaryllis she grew out at Christmas.

When the worst had happened, when a bulb of the foulest color had planted itself in May and was crowding, tearing, and working its way deeper instead of out, she found herself in Anna's kitchen reliving a much earlier time. Anna iced her heavy raisin bars while they were warm and set the pan on the trivet, and May broke them off on the fork lines and ate until she could eat no more, and scraped up the icing with her finger. "Save one for your husband," Anna said peaceably. Cole would come from the hospital. More and more May tried to be at Anna's when it was time for dinner. She knew Anna would call him; she liked Anna to be the one to let him in the door, his face ugly with grief.

For Cole there was no respite. But after school May parked in front of the house where she had grown up, now Anna's house, on the street of big Victorians. All but hers had been converted into student rooms; the MacLeods' place was a Young Life center. She climbed the steps to Anna's broad figure in the doorway, and complained like the child she had been when there was a chicken house in the back yard.

She complained about the past. About her father, his

overnight transfer to her, Anna, of his loyalty, his interests, himself. And then in old age his forgetting, his misplacing May's mother altogether. It relieved her to list these accusations.

Far from resenting her outbursts, Anna fell in with them. "Well, I don't know. Your mother had her own interests," she said, not at all averse to the subject, always ready to set foot firmly on old, delicate paths of memory. "And she was fond of so many. The young fellows. I do believe it hurt his pride."

"How do you know that?" May said rudely. Another thing about Anna as an old woman—she was in her eighties now—was that she would follow a thing to its root. Just as she would work her plump fingers down in the dirt and caress and fumble it without looking until it yielded the little potatoes tender as grapes that she used in her recipes, she would take a subject as far as anyone wanted to, with her blind, feeling, hardly curious mind. It might be she was as fearless, in that way, as May's mother had been in hers.

She would let fall in passing the most appalling secrets of the families whose children she had taught. She liked talk about the young, about May's daughters. They were her granddaughters, to her. She liked talk about sex. When May had told her, long ago, that Laura wanted to get married instead of going to college, Anna had said, "Well, if it's sex you'll never talk her out of it. And if you look at her, it is, you can see, she's got that mated-sheep look."

Sex, Anna always said decidedly, placidly, as if it were a fish she simply knew how to buy. May gazed at the voluminous cornflower-blue housecoat bent over the stove.

It's only Anna Olafsson here in your kitchen, who got up this morning out of the bed you brought out from Boston. It's 1978 now.

One of your grandchildren is dead. The boy. Carrie never had any boys. I had the boy. We named him Nicholas. Victory.

It's only Anna Olafsson, who taught us in the second grade.

As if she could make her mother understand this.

Anna lumbered up, turned on three burners, and set a pan on each. Looking at the gas where it burned blue, May thought one of the nice things about Anna was that she did not want you to get up and help. She unwrapped fish, cut chunks of butter. "We'll make all her favorites while she's here," Anna muttered as if to May's father, who had been dead two years.

"How do you know that?" May pressed. *Fond of so many.*

Anna would never say, "Well, your father told me, of course." She said instead, "Your mother had her crusades, dear." Then she said something May would have quarreled with before she learned you could never talk Anna out of one of her opinions, which she did not form empirically, from any evidence, but out of some phase of herself the way potatoes form eyes. Anna said, "Thank heavens you girls got his nature and not hers."

His nature. *"What do you mean?"* was all the force May could gather in opposition. Her son was dead, and all her force at that time was concentrated on pressing down the bulb inside her, the disbelieving horror—a bluish thing, a never-to-be-born thing that could not be prevented from growing—even when it was keeping still, half asleep, instead of tearing and rooting. It had starved out the layers that held her everyday obligations—which side of the yellow line to drive on, the groceries, her good manners—while exposing old, very old items that should have rotted into compost: her father's black suits, the carbolic smell of his car, his faithlessness. Oh, worse than any adultery of hers or anyone's: to simply forget the dead. "What do you mean, *his* nature?"

"Well, her *obsessions!*" snapped Anna, turning the big wedding ring set with pearls on her finger, startling May as she often did with her use of terms that sounded, in her Swedish accent, like crass slang. May had grown to like the pattern of Anna's speech, the shape she gave words with the horsy lower lip with its double selvedge rim that had fascinated May in the second grade. "You girls—both go-getters. You don't cry over spilt milk."

We don't what? What did you say?

"It was hard for your father," Anna went on. "Hard to carry on his shoulders. Poor girl, Anna Harkness"—hardly conscious it had been her own name for decades—"oh, she was up in the air. Change-the-world. Whereas your father . . . the world is what it is, to him." She still used the present tense, for May's father. "She. She never would be *happy*."

May waited a minute before speaking. Her mother singing "The Silkie," dancing into the furniture while enacting the silkie's emergence from the sea, her mother dancing to "Gentle Annie," making faces as she sang, " 'Now I stand alone 'mid the flowers, while they mingle their perfumes o'er thy tomb.' "

"But," she said at length, "we *were* happy. You can't say otherwise." That had a formal sound. "I mean we were as happy as anybody else, after the crash. How can you say that?"

"Not her. Not you," said Anna firmly. "Not when I had you. Not in my class. Now you asked me, dear. I don't think you had regular meals. And no sleep, and egged on at home to make it hard for yourself in the schoolyard. To run around like a calf with a heel fly. Now, of course, you're—"

"Oh, but I had you before the crash." May tried to keep her voice reasonable. "Really, what do you mean?"

"Oh, you came primed to speak up. Just the wrong thing

every time. You made an outcast of yourself. You lost your little friends. Isabel Barr."

"Isabel! But I don't remember that."

"Better not. Your sister would not associate with you, I'm ashamed to say. Mary Pitt couldn't do a thing with you."

I thought Isabel moved away, May thought. *She did move away.*

"You were a wild little thing, with your mama's full approval, when I got you in the second grade."

No more, she thought. What happened to me? "I was a silkie," she said.

Her mother was going down to the waterfront, where the hobos lived, to make a speech. Not the hobos, the unemployed. She was going to Hooverville to talk about the Unemployed Citizens' League.

Carrie said, "I don't see why I have to go. It's Saturday. I have to finish my application. I have to wash my hair. Couldn't just May go?" Carrie had "Blue Moon" on the phonograph; everyone was singing "Blue Moon."

"Neither one of you need go." Their mother was pulling up her ribbed stockings while she read the typescript laid out on the bedspread. She hurried to the mirror to put Vaseline on her red, chapped lips, which would be pleated all winter with little cuts from smiling.

"It's a stormy day to be going down to the tide flats," their father said as they came down, setting his bag on the hat rack bench and shaking out his overcoat. "There'll be mud."

"It's stopped raining."

"You're hoarse. You're coughing. You shouldn't go out. And

I can't pick you up, it's a first delivery, I'll be all afternoon and half the night."

"We'll take the streetcar back."

"I'm not at all easy about this, Anna."

"We will be perfectly safe."

"I'll take you down but I can't pick you up," he said again, scratching his head. "You must come out no later than four o'clock. And you're sure there will be police."

"You know they send someone when any of us speaks."

"Do you really want to go, May?"

No, she didn't want to go. "Yes," she said.

When he let them off it wasn't raining, the air was fresh and silvery. He rolled the wet window down to kiss her mother. "Be sensible, Anna."

Her mother laughed and patted her bag. "This is a sensible speech, John."

"I mean don't inflame them. And don't, whatever you do, smile. Don't even—don't look at them when you're speaking. These are men who—" Her father was almost pleading. "It would be like showing them food."

"Food," said her mother lightly, turning her back.

A wind sailed against them with its invisible load of water as they crossed the railroad tracks and started down Charles Street. There were no buildings to channel the wind, nothing but pier and open water beyond the acres of tin roofs in a kind of basin her mother said had been a shipyard. The street was not paved; already their boots were muddy.

"What are you going to say to them?" Now that it was too late to turn back.

Her mother steadied herself on May's shoulder and bent to pry mud from her boot heel with the tip of her umbrella. "Don't worry," she said. "I'm not going to go on and on, or even try to convince them, honestly. I'm leaving information that may be of use to them, that's all."

Smoke pouring from stovepipes ran into their noses and stung their eyes.

Now their boots were caked to the lace-hooks with the oily mud. Winding paths of mud led in and out among the shacks. From above May had gasped at how many there were. It was as if they had gone behind a curtain painted with buildings and streets into a huge fort in the open countryside, where men might appear in helmets, like the legions in her *Gallic Wars,* or around the next corner under blowing standards, spreading out maps.

Nobody appeared. Birds and wind made the only sounds. The place was not the huddle of tent poles and tarpaulins May had imagined but hundreds of wooden boxes, many of them raised on legs. Propped against the boxes were small, two-wheeled carts that made her think of the wagon she had pulled the chickens around in as a child. Where her mother turned downhill there was a box hut with a porch the width of two planks, three flat stones laid in a curve for a walk, and a picket fence. Everything here, the shacks in their hundreds, her mother said, had sprung up in just the two years since the city had the original place burned to the ground.

"Look at the gardens!" she said eagerly, seeing May glance at the little fence, but May refused to marvel, or give in and ask a question, she refused some acquiescence her mother wanted from her, some admission that her old childish longing at bedtime for everyone to be warm, fed, raised up where they had fallen, was only sleeping and not dead, now that she was in high school. Some word that she was still good.

"I'm glad you came with me," her mother said gaily.

A scrubby bush was growing everywhere, with the lower branches pruned away to give it the appearance of a small tree. They came to a clearing full of sawhorses and planks, with kerosene drums flattened into sheets covering cans of paint and turpentine.

Several dogs wandered after a big black malamute, sniffing under its blowing tail. A skeletal cat threaded its way through piles of sawdust and slipped under one of the shacks.

Her mother knew where to go. It was only two o'clock in the afternoon but the sky was a deep, charged gray, with white cloud on it pulled thin like cheesecloth. The waterfront was already darkening. Through the smoke May could smell water, or seaweed, on the wind, or it might have been the sewage the tide was taking out from the five privies built out over the water on stilts. May knew about these. Five privies for five hundred men. The men teetered out to them on long, rickety gangplanks, and at night some of them fell off drunk onto the rocks.

Soon the afternoon would be at an end. She would live through whatever would be said and done in the next two hours, and then forget it. With all that was imposed on her and chosen for her and unimportant, it would disappear from her life, her real, beginning life.

Tomorrow was Sunday, she had a lab report to write. Her father said she should think about medicine, when she told him she had given up her idea of being a writer in order to pursue chemistry. Whatever she chose, whatever happened to her, she would not be compelled as her mother was. No, she would not be pressed into errands like her mother's, unwanted mercies, hopeless schemes printed in leaflets.

In a little while she would go home, fall on her bed, lure from its hidden place inside her the look that had crossed Eugene's face when he got his test back and moved his thumb to cover the grade. She would think of how she might have comforted him, now that his shirts weren't starched and he couldn't concentrate because his father had lost everything. "The poor child," her mother said. Eugene a child! "His mother is Russian? And she came away from the Revolution?"

The lumberyard had closed down; Eugene's father had a job cleaning the hardware store and another delivering for the druggist.

May cast a final look at the sky. The water in the Sound was an olive color, almost black, with no light on the peaking ripples. The mountains could not be seen, the pure white Olympics. The trailing clouds were gone; dark, molded rain clouds were moving in. There was a damp freshness above the smoke and coming up from below it, from the wet soot in which the huts sat like a field of toadstools after rain.

There were places like this in other cities, with the same name: Hooverville.

In front of the mirror, fastening her barrettes, she had told herself that it would not be at all the way her mother hoped. The men would not be expecting them, or they would be drunk or begin telling the kind of jokes you could hear at school, or they would simply not be there, in the shack big enough for six to live in where they were supposed to gather to hear her mother speak.

But the men were none of these things. They were heavy-footed and slow coming in, like men after hard work. A dozen or so right away squatted and sat on the floor, then ten or fifteen more pushed in as voices swelled outside. The last to squeeze in lined the walls until no more would fit, removing their stocking caps with a precise, exaggerated politeness, but quickly pulling them back down over their ears. They kept their gloves on. It was icy November; you could see your breath in the cabin. The ones who couldn't fit in the room had the doorway and the narrow path to it blocked; there was no way you could get out now.

Sudden rain made a clatter on the tin roof and the men inside began to joke as water snaked down the wall behind May. At once the men standing outside hunched away, and the door was pulled shut.

While they were crowding onto the bunks, fishing in their pockets for tobacco, greeting each other warily, something sly settled over them, something May could feel. Some sour, ornery, restless expectation or wish.

"Ladies and gentlemen," her mother said hoarsely, over the rain, and only then did May see that another woman was in the room, on the edge of one of the bunks, a short woman sitting so erect she was swaybacked, with short bushy hair and a big forward jaw like a drawer left open. She had her son beside her. After a while May saw that she had one leg draped over his. It was not her son but a man even smaller than she who tapped out a cigarette on her thigh and lit it for her while the others jostled and crowded them on the bunk. Unperturbed, the small man said in a singsong out of the corner of his mouth, right over her mother's voice as though she weren't speaking, "Blackjack, Wing's place."

She didn't really listen to her mother. The rain released a strong smell of coffee grounds in the room, and of smoking lard, and now the air thickened as if those smells had been mixed with something a little sour, potash or chicken manure or old wet leaves raked up. The room had four bunks in it and a pile of bedrolls in the corner. There was a woodstove, unlit, made of bricks and coal-oil cans, with willow-pattern bowls just like the ones they had at home—maybe these were the ones from home— stacked on it, and a piece of ragged tin fashioned into a ladle. May had been given an upended washtub to sit on.

They had brought in a little plank table and placed a glass of water on it for her mother, and then a bowl of something that looked like an arrangement of pancakes, small, brown-edged, covered with flakes of black. "Like them cookies?" She jumped. A man in the front said, "Fried 'em on that there stove. Well? Eat 'em up." May smiled stupidly and nodded; she took one and bit into it. It was like a pancake but it had even less sugar and was filled with grit.

Her mother had been invited. The man who had invited her was shy and his English was not good, May knew, so he was not the one who was going to introduce her. May figured out who he was because he seemed to be the youngest, and he bowed to her mother and sent her quick, signaling looks, pulling his too-short, foreign- looking sweater sleeves down when she glanced at him. He was slight and nervous but apparently he was popular among the men. It appeared that certain leaflets he translated and tacked up were considered a harmless joke. It was a joke to be a Communist at his age. He had black hair growing down his neck and sad black eyes, thickly lashed. Despite his coloring, in a vague way he re- minded her of Eugene. He had the not-American nose, and carved, heavy, not-American lips.

The whole room seethed with scratching. *They have lice,* May said to herself with a sort of relish. She didn't want lice but she had no fear of them; her head had been full of them in the fourth grade. Half the grades had had them. Carrie, in the seventh and wearing curls, had wailed and stamped; her long hair had to be cut. But ripping the hairs between finger- and thumbnail to strip off the nits: that had been a savage pleasure.

Her mother had not been talking for very long when a noise began in the room that sounded like the barking of seals.

May saw that the men were spreading their jaws in vast, loud, anguished male yawns that bathed the folds under their eyes and made them work their jaws to bring their faces back into position. They passed the fervent yawns along and fell silent only when her mother began to cough. At that, as if she had finally talked sense, they bowed their heads and plunged their fingers into their beards.

To May's astonishment her mother was not speaking well. She kept hesitating and having to swallow, like a substitute at school. She drank repeatedly from the glass of cloudy water they had drawn for her from a tap by the sawhorses.

But eventually she steadied herself, threw her shoulders back. Her eyebrows drew together and that was a good sign. The rain had thinned to a plinking. May found she could let her own breath out.

Suddenly tears sprang to her mother's eyes, and with her hands she began to beckon and hush and urge the men in the room into some compact with her. She fixed her eyes on the ones in front who were listening, and stalked them until she was around in front of the little table, where there was hardly any room to stand, and she bent to the men sitting crosslegged on the floor and smoothed the air in front of them as if she were ironing. She was going into the litany May had heard so many times in their own living room, where it was possible to fall into a day-dream and not even hear.

The men had settled down; their hands lay on their knees and they slitted their eyes and let their heads hang sideways as if they were listening to the radio.

May lifted one foot and then the other off the floor; the rim of the washtub bottom had begun to bite into her legs. The leaking water was creeping toward the men. Her mother was losing her voice but didn't notice it; the words were pouring out of her now. "Why is there no bathhouse, when it would be easy to pipe water to a central building where you could bathe? That's what the Emergency Relief Administration *exists* for, does it not? Why must you rustle everything you need to live, gather your bedding and be afraid to hang it out to dry, tramp miles in search of things everybody must have by right? *By right,*" she hissed through clenched teeth, her big eyes almost popping. May looked away. Her mother dropped her voice. "What—kind—of government—do we live under?—that makes you afraid of anybody who comes down here, afraid of me? Afraid I'll put you on the tax rolls, or ship you out to labor camps. All over the country a hopeless quest is going on, not even for work anymore but for *food and warmth,* and going on in this city, in the rain, desperately! Ladies and gentlemen! *Cold rain!* Is there a human being who does not understand the words *cold rain?* And *who comes here?* The *government,* into your *one life,* and *burns your homes!*"

She looked straight at the young man who had invited her, who had flushed right to the neat, flat earlobes below his wool hat. "Oh, how hateful our country is!" she cried out. "How abominable. How it has cut men and women off in their one life. Our—motherland!" There she stopped, and smiled her wide flashing smile, and held up her arms despairingly, comically, her shirtwaist coming untucked. A few of the men smiled back, with what May saw was embarrassment for her in her disarray.

So that was what the little barrows were for. The men went out pulling wagons, the way May had when she collected things for her hideout in the chicken house. *One life.* The words, heavy as full buckets, settled in her. *One life. The one in this room. To wait to grow up . . . to grow up . . . and be sent back. To go out again pulling a wagon.*

Why live? May looked at the sharp tin ladle. You could cut your wrists. Did anyone here do that? *Why live? What kept you living, freezing and wet in a box on legs? Ugly, smelly, hidden from sight. What kept you living at all, going on and on, obedient, like a bobbin spinning with the thread used up? What were they all obeying? Was it no more than life? Just* life *made you do this? Life* made *you live?*

Her mother had paused. She closed her fingers around the glass and drank the last of the water. May waited, rubbing her cold hands in her lap.

They had put her behind her mother on the washtub by herself, facing the men. Every time she looked straight at them she felt her face burn. The cigarette smoke had made her eyes run. She had taken off her gloves to rub her eyes but she did not want them to think she was crying.

A man got to his feet, wobbling. "I'll tell you another thing, *ma'am.*" He pointed shakily at her mother. "We had all our *cats* . . . our *cats* to die." He rocked back on his heels as his friends steadied him. "Got sick, didn' they, boys? It was the city. Hadda bury sixty-some. What kind of a thing? You see what I mean? No cats, you got *rats.* Unsanitary. See that?"

"So they *done* it! Burned it down!" the big-jawed woman on the bunk shouted out in a surprising treble voice. "Got rid of the rats!"

"You may be right." Her mother was calm again, May could see. It did not worry her mother when she was in this state that a whole room was stirring, that men's eyes had begun to narrow and burn. Now she wanted them to say what they had been or done before they came here to live. That brought on a low growling in the room.

A man identified himself as a housepainter, and then a switchman spoke up, and several men who had been loggers. A man on the bunk said he had been a pipe fitter. A tall man lounging against the door broke in loudly. "Looky here. This here Filipine feller'll sew you a burlap bag. He'll make a goddamn bag and goddamn if somebody won't pay him for it." He put out his cowboy boot, with the little toe sticking out of a hole, and prodded a small man on the floor.

"I hap sewing machine," the man said cautiously, looking straight in front of him.

But they tired of this. They started grinning at each other. May was surprised that she could tell this while her mother did not seem able to: they were making things up. "I was a dance instructor," one said, crooking his little finger.

"Served a term in Congress, he did," called an old man with a squashed nose, jerking his thumb at the man with the cowboy boots. "Didn't ya?"

"Sexual congress," the man said, with his thumbs on his pocket flaps. This was a man May would have said was old, by his gray hair and drooping, wrinkled ears, but as she stared at him he unfolded his long legs and turned his boot at the ankle for the second time for her to see, as if his foot, and dirt and lice, and the smell of himself and the others in the room would have some secret appeal to her.

"Nice hat you got on," he said across the crowd, rubbing his chin seeded all over in silvery stubble. He shot a look out of his eyes at May as vivid as a sniff of turpentine. "Come over here a minute," he mouthed.

"No," she mouthed back, turning her head.

He was the one who came or was shoved forward at the end— there must have been a bet—and leaned down and kissed her mother. "Much obliged for the speech," he said. "Like you to have a token of my appreciation—" And wheezing he put his hand with the skin in bands like a chicken foot on hers, with his weight behind it to keep her wrist on the table. He cocked his matted head and pushed his lips out from under the mustache to meet hers. Her chapped sore lips. He made a loud, theatrical, smooching noise.

"Sir!" her mother said when he was done, with her free arm drawing May up from the washtub and close to her. "Here"— she smacked the papers—"is material for a meeting you may hold if you like, to organize this camp and demand what the city owes you, and if you don't want to do that, I leave it to you."

In the 1950s, when May took her own daughters to see Maureen O'Hara on the screen, proud and fiery but not forbiddingly pure, she would think of the men looking at her mother in that room, and of how carefully her mother had slid her arm out from under the man's until her hand met his and gripped it so that she could give it her strong handshake. How she stood up straight, and did not wipe off her lips where May could feel the kiss still printed, or show any recognition of the frog odor rising from the grooves of the man's corduroy, mixed with the smell of the bedrolls and of certain other men who had closed into a circle around them—a deep, burnt, throat-filling, vegetable smell that May had thought was moldy leaves until she identified it halfway through the meeting as urine, old urine.

The men who had closed in did not shake the hand her mother held out but fell back from her at that moment. It was over then. Ahead of them was only getting out, getting up the hill to the streetcar.

All of May's life, women speaking at rallies would say that moments like this one, when men fell back, showed the power of a woman of conviction. Yet it was bitter to her mother and May knew it, when they all stepped away from her and stopped listening, if they had been listening, and slumped again, and yawned. It brought her to tears.

Why did you do it, then? May cried silently. *Why do you have to?*

The young man, the Communist, walked with them a little way. He took her mother's hands and pressed them to his chest. "Thank you," he said in a whisper, shaking his head and grimacing. He was nothing but a boy, Carrie's age. "You see, we—you see"—but his strong lips twisted down at the corners and this May did not want to see, nor her mother raising her plaid sleeves to take the boy in her arms. But her mother was only loosening her bag to pull out an envelope. Why had May seen an embrace, an embrace turned from, though natural as a habit long established?

She decided to ask her mother. Tell me about that boy. I have a right to know. But she didn't do it that day; she never did it.

When she herself was old, May wondered if her mother knew all along that she had married a man who could forget her in a year. But why not forget? Why remember on and on? Why, instead of stopping, never stop?

Her mother closed the boy's hand around the envelope. "Listen to me. I promise you you'll get out of here. You'll work. I promise you." When they had gone a few steps she turned and called to him. "Kolya! Do you understand? Don't be afraid." He was standing there without waving.

"Charity is a trick," said May under her breath as they walked. She shrank from the look her mother gave her.

It was four o'clock, as they had promised her father, and now the west-facing walls were painted with a full wet brush of brass-color by the sun going down.

The mud sucked at their boots and two policemen at the top of the sidewalk waved at them, a mocking wave. May kept turning back to look at where they had been, and out at the water, which seemed not to move on the surface but only to shift from below like rice in a strainer. From above, the mud lay in veins of orange and lead-blue between the shacks. Now that she had been there May could see the dark forms of men everywhere, sitting on overturned crates and basins outside the doors.

"Why did they have us in that little place? Why didn't you just talk in the open, where the sawhorses were?"

"Because it rained all day. Because of the cold. They did it for us."

When they finally stopped walking May shook out her arms from the shoulder and pressed the fingers of her gloves tight. "Ugh!" She was thinking of the kiss.

She met her mother's eyes, each with its one deep line under it like a chair rocker. They were the same height, but May was still growing. Soon she would look down on her mother. Her mother began to smile as if she were thinking the same thing. She got one of her brown lozenges out of its paper and she took May's hand in her own cold ones as if she were going to ask a favor that would be hard to grant, as if she were already comforting a daughter who could not grant it.

"That's not the way I would choose to give or get a kiss, my darling, but it was no different than if—oh, Dr. Thorp did it. Poor man, he's going to get my cold." Her forehead had purple ridges under the streetlight, her beautiful mouth shrank to two dark, irregular marks as she coughed.

May was suddenly weak and tired, and she wanted, as she almost never did anymore, to lean on her mother or be held in her arms, but the streetcar was coming. And then in the streetcar when they sat down her mother reached for her gloved hand, but May did not want the touch by then, and she took her hand back. Her mother held the bar in front of them. For a long time her thumb plied it as if she might bring a spark out of it.

May put her head back on the seat and let her eyes roll against her half-closed lids. It was getting dark. Before she slept she saw her mother as she always would, a thin woman blanched by the bulbs in the ceiling of the car, who looked like a tired student on the University Line, biting her lips and making notes on the back of a leaflet pressed on her bag where the ghosts of words from her pencil point were swarming on the leather, with the battery of her hair winking on and off in the dim light. She looked up each time someone got on, and the expression on her face smoothed into the one the man in the camp had taken for something that would let him kiss her, something lenient and unexacting.

Something—despite her endless hunt for the lair of justice, despite all she lived to overthrow—that said, *should life be otherwise?* It seemed to May to be the very look on the face of the seal that had come up and gazed at them, a long look of curiosity almost tender, before it slipped from the rock into water that ran together and hid it from the ones looking back.

About the Author

Valerie Trueblood grew up in Virginia. Her writing has been published in *The Iowa Review, One Story, Northwest Review*, and elsewhere. She is a contributing editor of *The American Poetry Review* and serves as cotrustee of the Denise Levertov Literary Trust. She and her family live in Seattle.